THE LAST FLIGHT

JEN TALTY

Jupiter Press

THE LAST FLIGHT

AN AEGIS NETWORK NOVELLA

the SARICH BROTHERS series
book 3 of 5

Ramey's Story

**USA Today Bestselling Author
JEN TALTY**

"Deadly Secrets is the best of romance and suspense in one hot read!" *NYT Bestselling Author Jennifer Probst*

"A charming setting and a steamy couple heat up the pages in an suspenseful story I couldn't put down!" *NY Times and USA today Bestselling Author Donna Grant*

"Jen Talty's books will grab your attention and pull you into a world of relatable characters, strong personalities, humor, and believable storylines. You'll laugh, you'll cry, and you'll rush to get the next book she releases!" Natalie Ann USA Today Bestselling Author

"I positively loved *In Two Weeks*, and highly recommend it. The writing is wonderful, the story is fantastic, and the characters will keep you coming back for more. I can't wait to get my hands on future installments of the NYS Troopers series." *Long and Short Reviews*

"*In Two Weeks* hooks the reader from page one. This is a fast paced story where the development of the romance grabs you emotionally and the suspense keeps you sitting on the edge of your chair. Great characters, great writing, and a believable plot that can be a warning to all of us." *Desiree Holt, USA Today Bestseller*

"*Dark Water* delivers an engaging portrait of wounded hearts as the memorable characters take you on a healing journey of love. A mysterious death brings danger and intrigue into the drama, while sultry passions brew into a believable plot that melts the reader's heart. Jen Talty pens an entertaining romance that grips the heart as the colorful and dangerous story unfolds into a chilling ending." *Night Owl Reviews*

"This is not the typical love story, nor is it the typical mystery. The characters are well rounded and interesting." *You Gotta Read Reviews*

"*Murder in Paradise Bay* is a fast-paced romantic thriller with plenty of twists and turns to keep you guessing until the end. You won't want to miss this one..." *USA Today bestselling author Janice Maynard*

To my brother, Jeff Holbrook. Thank you for your service!

WELCOME TO THE AEGIS NETWORK

The Aegis Network is the brainchild of former marines, Bain Asher and Decker Griggs. While serving their country, Bain and Decker were injured in a raid in an undisclosed area during an unsanctioned mission. Instead of twiddling their thumbs while on medical leave, they focused their frustration at being sidelined toward their pet project: a sophisticated Quantum Communication Network Satellite. When the devastating news came that neither man would be placed on active duty ever again, they sold their technology to the United States government and landed on a heaping pot of gold and funded their passion.

Saving lives.

The Aegis Network is an elite group of men and women, mostly ex-military, descending from all branches. They may have left the armed forces, but the armed forces didn't leave them. There's no limit to the type of missions they'll take, from kidnapping, protection detail, infiltrating enemy lines, and everything in between, no job is too big or small when lives are at stake.

As Marines, they vowed no man left behind.

As civilians, they will risk all to ensure the safety of their clients.

A NOTE FROM JEN TALTY

Some researchers have said there is a correlation between the ocean and being calm, happier, and more creative. Having spent a winter in Jupiter, Florida, I'd say these researchers are right on the money.

the SARICH BROTHERS series was born while I spent four months in Jupiter, walking the beach, visiting the Jupiter Lighthouse, driving around Jupiter Island, dining at various places on the water, and overall enjoying this next chapter in my life known as 'empty nest'.

The Sarich Brothers, while poor, had a good life, raised by loving parents. However, their father was killed in the line of duty when the oldest boy was just twenty and the youngest fourteen, changing their lives forever...

Each of the brothers struggle with a restlessness, in part caused by their father's death. They are strong, honorable, and loyal men. They aren't looking for a woman, as their jobs aren't necessarily conducive with long-term relationships. It's going to take an equally strong woman to rip down the Sarich Brothers defenses and help them settle their restlessness, so they can give their hearts.

The series does not need to be read in order, but the four novellas do follow a timeline.

Come join each of the Sarich boys in their journey to heal old wounds, mend broken hearts, and find their way to true happiness with the love of a good, strong woman.

I want to add that since this series has been released, and then re-released, my readers, have begged me to write Mrs. Sarich's story...well, it's coming! Look for Catherine's story, THE MATRIARCH, in 2020.

Sign up for Jen's Newsletter (https://dl.bookfunnel.com/rg8mx9lchy) *where she often gives away free books before publication.*

Join Jen's private Facebook group (https://www.facebook.com/groups/191706547909047/), where she posts exclusive excerpts and discusses all things murder and love!

BOOK DESCRIPTION

Ramey Sarich graduated from West Point Military Academy with honors and a broken heart. Swearing off relationships, but not women, he dives into his career as a test pilot for the Army. He's cocky, lives on the edge, but he knows he's the best test pilot the Army has ever seen. So, when one of the planes he's testing nearly crashes, he doesn't believe it was an accident. Wanting an outside source, he contacts his brothers and they send help in the form of an ex-military female pilot now part of the AEGIS NETWORK. Ramey is prepared for anything, except Tequila Ryder.

Tequila Ryder has spent the last few years raising her half-sister's son. Now that he's settled in college, Tequila is eager to jump back in the field with the AEGIS NETWORK. She's dealt with more than one arrogant pilot before, however, Ramey is anything but typical and as she dives into the investigation she can only come to two conclusions.

Either someone is trying to destroy Ramey's career.

Or kill him.

...together they unravel a twisted plot, while entangling their hearts, and falling hard. Hopefully they won't crash and burn both in the sky, and in love.

PROLOGUE

Nothing felt better than flying upside down in a sixth-generation jet fighter, testing the limits of new technology. The nose of the plane cutting through the air like a sharp carving knife gliding through a perfectly cooked medium-rare steak.

The howling sound of the hydraulics system slowly disabling echoed in the cockpit.

"Fuck," Captain Ramey Jordan Sarich muttered.

The plane bucked left, and he hit the comms button. "Engine one is out." He shut the power down. The controls rattled in his hands. A loud tearing of metal screeched across the night sky.

"Engine two is out." Ramey tried to restart the engines, but nothing. He pulled the nose up, rolling five degrees to his right and toward a section of the desert he might be able to land this sucker without killing himself, and destroying a fifty-million-dollar plane.

"Total engine failure."

This would be his second crash in three weeks, and he didn't think the United States Government would appreciate the loss of the aircraft.

Nor the money it cost to build such a prototype.

"Starting protocol for an emergency landing," he said. He'd been a test pilot for the Army for the last five years, and in that time, he'd only lost one plane, three weeks ago, when the cargo hold of the newest sixth-generation Stealth Bomber caught fire. Typically, when testing an aircraft, it wasn't loaded with firepower. Only that particular test run wasn't just about the plane, but the weapons system as well.

Less than a minute after he'd ejected from the bomber, it exploded, sending shrapnel flying danger-ously close to his body.

His thigh ached, remembering the fourteen stitches that were required on his leg because a hunk of metal had pierced his muscle.

"Six miles from the runway and I won't make it. I will be landing three miles southeast." Just as he finished his statement, he lost all power and needles on his instruments spun out of control. The plane went eerily dark. Talk about flying blind. A pilot was taught to trust his mechanisms, not his gut because, in the air, your feelings lied. It didn't matter how good of a pilot you were, you could be flying level, but your body said you were leaning five degrees to the right.

Thankfully, the moon and the stars lit up the desert sky. He eyed the runway at White Sands Missile Range in New Mexico. He knew exactly the best place to land this sucker but wasn't sure he'd make it to that spot either. Not only that, he'd be landing a flying brick considering he had no way to slow down or speed up. Most likely he'd come in so hot that the nose would plunge into the ground, flipping the tail overhead, flames erupting shortly after that.

As he gripped the controls, the plane violently vibrated, and he could hear his mother say, "Eject! It's just a plane."

But equally loud, he could hear the United States Government screaming at him to save the technology.

"Sorry, mom," he whispered as the ground raced up like a panther chasing after its prey. He'd landed more than one aircraft in an emergency. He just hoped this wouldn't be the one that ended it all, and that he saved as much of the equipment as possible if not all of it.

The Army's fire trucks raced across the desert, lights helping to guide him to the safest place to land. His chest tightened as adrenaline roared through him, keeping his emotions from seeping too far into his psyche. Sure, a bit of fear kicked in. He'd be insane if he didn't have a healthy dose of mortality.

Crazy, he wasn't.

However, most would say he flirted with disaster.

He readily agreed.

With all his might, he held the nose up, and as soon as the wheels bounced on the rough ground, he punched the manual breaks. The wings tipped, scraping the desert as the plane barreled forward, seemingly not slowing down at all.

It took another five minutes of white knuckling the controls until the jet fighter came to a sudden stop, the nose dropping into the desert sand, lurching his body forward, only to have his harness yank him back.

He hated whiplash.

Following protocol, he went through his checklist, looking at everything with a watchful eye. He pulled the flight box out of the compartment, which he'd review with his boss. As a test pilot, a lot went wrong with his flights, and that was expected. But three weeks ago, he believed someone fucked with his plane, even if the government didn't. Based on the chain of events leading up to his emergency landing tonight, he knew something wasn't as it seemed.

Time to call in his brothers.

He climbed from the plane, noting the slight tremble in his body. Some referred to him as being reckless. The kind of man who took unnecessary risks.

Or perhaps he had a death wish.

He'd give the world reckless. But, he did whatever it took to get the job done, and he got paid to put his life on the line, something he never questioned.

"What the hell happened up there?" Lieutenant Colonel Jasper Marlin asked? Marlin, as bosses go, wasn't half bad, but he also didn't have much of a backbone when it came to pushing the higher ups.

"I lost both engines without any warning."

"Engine failure isn't uncommon."

Ramey did his best to contain his frustration by sucking in a deep breath and letting it out slowly. "The aircraft went completely dark. Had I been above ten thousand feet, I would have fallen from the sky." He ranked his hand through his hair. "Someone fucked with that plane."

"Since when are you paranoid? Besides, do I need to remind you how often things go wrong on your test flights? Isn't that why we do this? Figure out the problem so we can make sure we've got the—"

Ramey held up his hand. "I don't need the politically correct response to what happened. I need answers, and I need a favor."

Jasper peered over his dark-rimmed glasses. "Why do I get the feeling I'm not going to like this?"

"I want you to bring in the organization my two older brothers work for to investigate both accidents."

"The Aegis Network, right?"

"That's the one." Ramey rubbed the scruff on his face as he glanced around. "I want them to have access to all the reports."

"That's going to be tough."

"But you can make it happen."

Jasper shook his head. "I can order an independent investigation, but it can't be by anyone with the last name Sarich, no matter how good your brothers are."

"They'd send someone else."

"You realize if I do this that I'm going to have to ground you?"

Ramey nodded. The last thing he wanted was to be benched. Flying was more than his job. It was his passion. "Are you going to make the call, because if you don't, I'm going to hire them myself."

"I'll see what I can do."

Ramey didn't have any enemies, that he knew of.

But someone either wanted to ruin his career or wanted him dead.

Or both.

1

*T*equila Ryder sat in the recon room at the White Sands Missile Range going over the crash report of Captain Ramey Sarich's first incident. There wasn't much left of the plane, but the Army's report, what she'd been allowed to read, indicated mechanical failure and thus far, no pilot error.

The weapons system, however, the information was blurry. The government had been creating new technology and new ways to decimate the enemy. She'd been given only the bare specs on the flight where Ramey had been forced into an emergency landing and nothing on any other tests. Something she needed her bosses, Bain Asher and Decker Griggs at the Aegis Network to fix.

Ramey's flight had been the new weapons first live test run. Everything had gone as planned until the bay doors opened without Ramey engaging them, or so Ramey had said. The flight recorder confirms he did not use the commands to engage the weapons, but that didn't mean anything, and she suspected there was more to that story than the government was giving her.

Or Ramey.

She tossed the folder on the table, leaning back, stretching her arms up over her head and stared at the ceiling. Ramey had attended West Point, and she had attended the Air Force Academy. They graduated the same year, and their careers had followed a similar path in the sense that when she retired, she'd been a test pilot as well. She never intended to retire at such a young age, barely getting her career off the ground, but two years ago, when her half-sister was diagnosed with terminal cancer, she didn't look back.

Her nephew, Grant, had been seventeen when his mother passed, only two years after his father had died. Grant needed her and no way would she let her sister down, not after everything she'd sacrificed so Tequila could have the opportunities she had after their father had died. It was the least she could do, and now that Grant was doing well at the Air Force Academy, Tequila felt she could get her career back on track, even if it wasn't in the military anymore.

She lifted her wrist and glanced at her smartwatch.

Ramey was ten minutes late.

Tardiness was not in her wheelhouse, and she hated it when anyone made her wait.

She stood, making her way across the room with a half-full mug of crappy, cold coffee, contemplating if she should dump it out, or warm it up.

"Tequila? Her fucking name is Tequila?" a husky male voice rang out from down the hallway.

She glanced over her shoulder at who she assumed to be Ramey standing near the door. He had sandy brown hair, dark complexion, and one hell of a sexy, scruffy face. It wasn't a five o'clock shadow, nor was it a full-grown beard. He was manly perfection wrapped in a flawless package of lean muscle. Leaning against the coffee station, she cocked her head to hear better and reminded herself she was on the job, not at the local watering hole during happy hour.

"It's seriously not a nickname? Christ, Logan, who the fuck did you send to help me, a God damned Margarita? How can I take this chick seriously?"

This wouldn't be the first time someone made fun of her name, and she was sure it wouldn't be the last. Could have been worse considering her sister's name was Rum.

"When I meet her all I'm going to be able to think about is sprinkling salt on her, licking her, drinking her, then sucking on a lemon. She better be hot on the eyes, or I'm coming after you, bro." He tapped his phone, then turned in her direction, taking maybe three steps before pausing with his mouth gaping wide-open.

"Sexy enough for you?" she asked, batting her eyelashes and fluffing her long, straight blonde hair. "I know the boobs are a little on the small side, but my ass makes up for it if you're an ass man. Oh, and my belly button is great for shots." She'd always had a sassy mouth, which often got her in trouble, but she couldn't help herself when it came to her name.

He scratched the side of his face as he entered the conference room. "I take it you're Tequila Ryder?" With his hands on his hips, he stopped in front of her and looked her up and down. The corners of his mouth tipped upward. "Turn around."

"What?" God, she'd spent all of a minute with this guy, and she wanted to know more about him. Something about the way he carried himself with a cool confidence and a subtle, but noticeable sweetness, made her want to hand him a saltshaker.

"I'm an ass man, so I want to check yours out."

"You're an asshole, is what you are." She drew her lips into a tight line, pulling in a smile. Sparring with a man, especially one that looked like Ramey, was almost as much fun as doing a fly-by.

He tossed his hands wide. "Hey, you brought up your ass, not me."

He had a point.

If she'd met him in a bar, flirting would take on a whole new meaning.

But she was standing in an Army Base, and she was on the job.

"Why don't you tell me why you think someone messed with your test runs?"

She tried not to eye his ass when he strolled in front of her and poured himself a cup of coffee. His thick biceps flexed as he tilted the pot.

"Because nothing went wrong until it all went wrong and rule of—"

"Rule of Seven dictates that there must be seven events before a catastrophe," she said as she raised her mug. "Retired Air Force Test Pilot."

He arched a brow. "You don't say."

She clanked her mug against his. "Why weren't you grounded after the first incident?"

He shrugged. "The weapon system had never been tested in flight before, and I was told that the second I flipped the switch to manual launch a wire tripped, creating a spark and the rest is history."

"Were you really testing a weapons system?"

"Only one piece." He set his mug down, resting his ass on the table, folded his arms across his chest, and glanced down the hallway. "What wasn't in any of those reports is that the plane was also a sixth-generation plane. There are only two prototypes."

She cocked her head. "The second incident wasn't a stealth bomber?"

"Neither incident was." He shook his head. "Same body frame, but I assume they didn't tell you that and just gave you the specs on the current model."

"They gave some of the modifications for the test, but no. How wicked are the sixth-generation planes?"

"Fucking awesome, if I can keep them from killing me."

She set her mug down. Not only did the planes intrigue her, but so did Ramey. "Why'd the government hire me if they aren't going to give me all the information?"

"Because I asked my boss to have an independent evaluation."

"Thus far, based on what I've read, I'd have to agree with the Army's findings and that both incidents were caused by mechanical failure, but that's based on incorrect information. I'm sure they've looked at it with all the correct specs and found the same thing. Otherwise, you'd be standing in front of a review board."

"Someone messed with my planes," he said with a clipped tone. "And someone is covering it up."

"What makes you so sure about that?" She didn't think for one second that Ramey was the kind of man that would want an independent investigation when he'd been cleared unless he knew something.

The question was: what did he know and why was he keeping it from her?

"What if I told you that two other test flights were messed with, only I caught the problem before it happened."

"Did you report them?"

"No. The first time was a week before the crash. Grey tape was used on the rivets instead of orange tape while servicing the engine. Had I not inspected the plane and removed the tape, well, bad shit would have happened. That said, it's a mistake that has been made before when people don't follow standard operating procedures."

"Are you big on them?"

"I wrote the book on SOP's."

She nodded. "Do you have the names of everyone who worked on that plane between runs?" During her days as a pilot, one of her pet peeves had been those who didn't think they needed to use the checklist. SOP's were created to make sure planes didn't go down, and that good people don't die.

"I do."

"All right, and the other time?"

"A week before this last flight. When I started the engines, they didn't sound right. Made a coughing noise, if you know what I mean."

"I know that noise."

"I delayed the run and found there was a small tear in the oil hose."

"Split or cut?" she asked. Things went wrong all the time, but this did seem over the top for one test pilot.

"Looked split, but who knows." He looped his arm over her shoulder.

She glanced between his hand and his face, which sported the most adorable grin she'd ever seen. It was a cross between an innocent little boy and a man who knew precisely what a woman wanted.

Dangerous combination.

"I keep journals of all my test runs back at my place. Maybe you can find something I missed."

"I don't think the United States Army would appreciate you keeping personal records."

"I won't tell if you don't." He nudged her hip. "Let's

go back to my place. I took my bird in, and it's a nice day for a chopper ride."

"You've got your own helicopter?"

"Two of them, actually. Along with three other planes, one that I built myself."

"Nice." She ignored the fact that he planted his hand firmly on the small of her back as they made their way through the Depot and out into the hot, desert air. Everyone said that a hundred-degree day in dry heat was nothing like eighty degrees in humidity.

Liars.

It was hotter than black pavement on bare feet.

They crossed through a parking lot toward the hangar, his hand still touching her back and frankly, she liked it.

A little too much.

As they approached the hangar, she spied a relatively new, bright orange, luxury Bell Jetranger. "Nice ride," she said.

"Just bought it a couple of months ago."

"You going to let me fly her?"

"We haven't even gotten naked together, and you expect me to let you fly one of my babies? I think not." He tossed her a headset he'd snagged from the cockpit.

"And if I took off all my clothes, then could I fly her?"

He arched a brow. "You just want to touch my controls."

"In your dreams." She winked, adjusting her mouthpiece. "I'm all about the machine, not the man."

He laughed. "So, you'd get naked just to be in the pilot seat."

"I don't need to be when you've got duel controls." She climbed in and adjusted the harness.

"The way you say that it sounds kinky." His throaty voice boomed in her ears as he flipped a few switches, which engaged the engine and the blades. Nothing sounded better than the whop whop of the hydraulic system kicking into action. The helicopter rattled, and her body tingled with anticipation.

Being in the air was almost better than sex.

Almost.

Ramey buckled himself in, gave the thumbs up to the crew on the ground before saluting and taking the controls into his hands. The bird lifted with ease thirty feet off the ground before the nose dipped slightly and Ramey engaged the throttles, propelling the bird upward, and punched forward.

Her fingers itched to take the controls as they flew low and fast across the desert. "Where is your place, exactly?"

"Ten miles dead ahead."

Chung! Click!

She leaned to her right, glancing over her shoulder. The tail end of the chopper swung left and right as the rotor blade wobbled, vibrating the tail.

"Shut rotor off," she commanded.

"Done," he said with a tight voice. "You've got comms and navs because—"

A loud popping noise, followed by the aircraft

jerking violently interrupted his words. She sprang into action, flipping the dashboard controls to her side of the helicopter.

"Shut comms off."

"No mayday?" she questioned, though she hadn't planned on calling it in. Not yet, anyway.

"Fuck," Ramey muttered. "Shut engine one down."

She didn't ask why just did as he instructed. She'd never liked being a co-pilot because she wasn't in control, but by the thick, black smoke coming from the engine, she wasn't about to argue.

"We need to land this bird now," she said.

"See that building in front of us?"

"I do."

"That's home. Let's do our best to get us as close as we can."

"You live in a tin hangar?" She glanced around in search of a house, but all she saw was a hunk of metal and desert.

The helicopter bucked left.

"Losing pressure in engine two," she said. "Shutting it down."

"Going to be a rough landing," Ramey said.

The chopper rattled, and the only sound that filtered through the desert was the blade cutting unevenly through the air.

"Have you ever landed controlling the blades?"

"A few times," she said as she reached for the level that controlled autorotation.

Ramey handled the rest of the controls with the

skills of a master pilot. Even she was impressed, and that was hard to do.

"Take it a little slower," he said as he pulled the nose up, pushing the aft of the chopper down and propelling them into a slight hover. "Feel the shimmy?"

The helicopter bucked left and right, rattling her teeth. She twisted the lever, slowing the spinning action of the blades, the vibration dangerously close to allowing the blades to break from the helicopter.

"Shut it down now," he said.

She pulled back and disengaged the power manually.

"Brace for impact," Ramey said calmly.

The ground came up a little too quickly, and the skeets bounced off the sand, punching the aircraft back up before Ramey brought it down again, this time, they skidded before coming to a halt.

She twisted, looking at the spinning blades, which wobble as they slowed. "Rear rotor, double engine failure, and main prop going off axis? You're either cursed or—"

"Someone is trying to kill me."

2

*R*amey wasn't sure what made him more nervous, the fact he'd been in another emergency landing.

Or having a woman in his house.

He pulled back the large metal door to the hangar and his home. It screeched like fingers across a chalkboard, a noise he'd gotten used to over the last five years.

"Ladies first," he said, stepping aside, waving his hand out in front, just like his father had taught him when he'd gone on his first car date. Ramey swallowed the thick emotion that teetered on the edge of spewing like a volcano every time he thought about his father. "Straight back to that orange door over there." Ramey had been sixteen and a Junior in high school when his father had died. The date not only marked his father's passing but the day he'd received his nomination to West Point.

However, his father died before Ramey could tell him the good news.

"Impressive flying machines you have." She reached her hand out, letting her fingers glide across the nose of Roxi, his pride and joy. "How long did it take to build this one?"

"Seven months."

"I'm impressed." The corners of Tequila's mouth tilted upward in a sultry smile. "I'm building one now, but I think it will take me a little longer."

"Nothing better than flying something you made with your own two hands."

She nodded. "Anyone else have access to this place? Family? Friends? Girlfriends?"

"Not really," he said, nudging her forward. In the five years he'd lived in this hunk of tin, he'd never had a woman inside, not even his mother, two sisters-in-law, nor his two-month-old niece. Of course, living in the middle of a desert where there is only a dusty dirt road or the friendly skies to bring visitors, made it difficult.

Besides, his father would roll over in his grave if he didn't go home as often as he could, and that was something Ramey prided himself on.

"No ex-girlfriends with an ax to grind?"

"You're the first female to ever see the inside of this joint."

She glanced toward him as he rested his hand on the curve of her back. Her straight blonde hair flowed over her shoulders like a cascading waterfall of all things beautiful. Her big, brown eyes carried the kind of confidence and strength that came with hard knocks, something he admired.

"That doesn't mean there isn't a scorned woman out there wanting to—"

"The few women I've dated where things might have ended on not so good terms, wouldn't know how to find me."

"And women you've dated from the base?"

"For the record, I've dated only one woman in the Military, and that was back when I attended West Point." Bile rose from his stomach, smacking the back of his throat. It had been years since he even uttered her name.

Denise.

His skin prickled.

"Besides, all the incidents happened on base, including the one we just experienced."

"We don't know that until we've examined all the evidence."

He lowered his chin as he reached for the door, catching a glimmer in her gaze.

"There are civilian women on the base that could have gained access to your plane." She cocked her head. "Are you telling me you've never had a relationship of any kind with a woman or two on the base?"

"Are you suggesting I'm a player?" He unlocked the door that led into the living quarters. He'd bought the hangar and land surrounding it from an older man who'd reluctantly sold it at the begging of his granddaughter.

Ramey couldn't contain a half smile at the thought. Good looking and a smart woman.

"I know your type," Tequila said as she stepped into the foyer.

All of a sudden, his pulse raced with something akin to nervousness.

Ramey didn't get nervous.

Ever.

"And what type is that?" His living quarters weren't vast with one bedroom, one bathroom, a large family room, and a galley kitchen, but he liked to think he had excellent decorating skills with his dark brown bomber-leather furniture against a white-washed wood floor. A built-in bookcase lined the back-wall with his collection of Ray Bradbury books and family photos displayed proudly.

"Wow. Nice digs and not what I would have expected from a guy like you."

"You don't know a thing about me." He waltzed toward the kitchen, stomping his feet. Not only did he feel as though aliens had invaded his personal space, but he prided himself on being aloof.

If his mother were here, she'd grab his ear.

"Wanna bet?"

He was about to tell Tequila no, but she kept talking.

"You're cocky and arrogant, but you're also smart. You're good at what you do, but you constantly push the limits, and you like living on the edge. You play as hard as you work, but you don't do relationships and have never had a long-lasting girlfriend."

"Wrong," he said, then snapped his mouth shut, ducking his head into the fridge, pulling out two beers. What was the big deal about letting her think he'd never been in love? Hell, even his brothers didn't know about Denise. The only one who knew had been his mother and not until after the fact.

"What do I have wrong?" She held up a picture of him with his brothers taken at Logan's wedding.

"I've been in a serious relationship." He handed her a beer while he chugged half of his before taking the image from her hand. "My brothers," he said. "But you've meet Logan and Nick."

"This was recent? I've never met your brother's families or your other brother." She held up a family portrait taken just a couple of weeks ago.

He tapped the picture with his forefinger. "My mom and next to her is my sister-in-law, Mia, who is married to Logan and that's their little girl, Abigail. That tall one at the end is baby Dyl or Dylan. And next to him is Nick and his very pregnant wife, Leandra, who is about to pop any day now."

"Nick took a bunch of time off work. My boss tells me he's a nervous wreck about the whole baby birthing thing."

"He is." Ramey shook his head.

She took a small sip of her beer. "So, tell me about this long-lasting affair."

"No." The word came out of his mouth fast, hard, and cold.

"That explains a lot."

"What the hell does that mean?"

She shrugged. "You got burned, and now you live the life of going from one short-term fling to the next." She patted his shoulder. "You and I are similar. I've never had a serious relationship, and I never plan on having one, but I've never been burned."

He sat on the sofa and stared at her as she eyed all the books and photos on his shelves. She'd pegged him pretty quickly, and the only thing he knew for sure about her was that she was confident and reacted calmly under pressure.

"Don't you want to get married? Have kids?"

She tilted her head back and laughed. The sound rolled through the air like hot fudge being drizzled over ice cream. "I don't need to be married to have a child, and I don't see myself getting married because the entire concept of a wedding gives me the willies."

"I thought all girls dreamed of the big wedding and white dress."

"Not this girl. Nope." She sat down in the chair across from him. Leaning back, she crossed her legs. "I won't be a man's property, and I'm no virgin."

"What about having a life partner?"

She arched a brow. "Do you want one?"

At one point in his life, he wanted it all.

Then Denise happened.

"Not particularly, no."

She raised her glass. "Cheers to being single."

He followed her gesture and took a long gulp. "I have to ask, why'd your parents name you Tequila?"

"My grandmother's maiden name was Whiskey. She and my dad made a bet on the Super Bowl the year my sister was born. My dad lost, and he had to name his kids after whiskey. My sister's name is Rum."

"I think I just fell a little in love with your grandmother."

"She was something special."

Any other time or place, he'd be working his charm on Tequila. With her refreshing attitude regarding relationships, he figured they'd have to be compatible in bed.

However, someone was messing with his planes, and he needed her help, and he never fucked people he worked this closely with.

And certainly not in his home.

"So, are we going to talk about what happened with my chopper an hour ago?" he asked, needing to get his focus off the way she twirled her hair, wrapping it between her fingers, swirling the strands.

"We both saw the cable to the rotor and how clean the tear was, so I believe it was no accident, but we'll know more once my equipment gets here and I can run some tests."

"But you can't run those same tests on the Government planes." He scratched the side of his face, the growth of five days of not shaving tingled across his fingertips. While he didn't spend a lot of time with the crew and his co-workers, he got along with everyone. He treated those who serviced the planes with the utmost respect.

They deserved it.

He went out of his way to be kind and considerate to everyone on the team because his life depended on them. Contrary to popular belief, he didn't have a death wish, only hovering on edge made him feel more alive than anything else. His two older brothers had found a balance in their lives with their wives, filling a void created by tragedy. Logan described it as coming home. Nick described it as finding himself again.

Ramey didn't feel lost. Or broken. Or disconnected from himself. He did feel a restlessness that nothing, not even flying, filled.

His senior year at West Point, that sensation dissipated in the form of a warm female classmate. Denise had made him feel alive in ways he didn't know existed until she left him standing in the courthouse with a marriage license in his hand. It had taken him a long time to get over Denise, and he was over her.

But he'd never put himself in such a vulnerable position again. It just wasn't worth it.

"Probably not, but I'm going to set up interviews with the crew members that worked on both planes. I'm good at reading people."

He had to give her that.

"We'll need to request the security—"

"I already asked for the cameras on the tarmac, but

seriously that cable could have been cut two days ago before the rotor came apart."

Again, she was right.

Nothing sexier than a smart woman.

"What another beer?" he asked.

She nodded. "And maybe something to eat? I'm starving."

"I can make you a turkey sandwich."

"Perfect."

Now he was making a woman food in his house. If he weren't careful, he'd be showing her his bedroom.

Now that was a scary thought.

"And what about those notes? The entire reason you brought me here," she said as she glided across the room like steam floating off a lake.

"I'll get them in a second." He pulled out a bag of turkey, lettuce, tomato, cheese, mustard, and mayo out of his fridge along with two more beers. "Unless you want to make us a couple of sandwiches and I'll go get my files."

"Works for me," she said.

"I'll be right back." He left in his kitchen, feeling a combination of excitement and fear, which reminded him of ever test flight.

Damn. Now he was comparing women to flying. Dangerous thinking.

He flicked the switch on the wall, and immediately his bedroom lit up. Even though he'd never had a woman in his room, always spending the night with them, he kept his room tidy and clean. His king size dark cherry bed perfectly made with the corners tucked in just right like his mother had taught him, stared back at him under the skylights.

After Denise, he'd never brought a woman home. One of his many odd rules, but it kept him from falling so hard for a woman he couldn't see straight. And yet, here he was, with an incredibly beautiful woman, named Tequila, and his only thought was how nice she'd look naked in his bed.

He blinked a few times and then snagged the files from his desk. He turned and walked right into her.

"What are you doing?" he asked, the folder falling from his fingertips as she wrapped her sweet hands around his neck.

"Getting this out of the way so we can work together to find out who is trying to kill you."

Before he could blink, her soft, pink lips brushed against his. Her tongue pushed into his mouth, probing every inch. He grabbed her by the hips and broke off the kiss.

"Getting a kiss out of the way? Or is it more like me tossing you on that bed and lets really get it out of the way."

"I'd say the latter is good."

3

Everything about Ramey sent a warm sizzle across Tequila's body like butter melting on hot toast.

He grabbed her thighs, hoisting her up as she wrapped her legs around his waist, clasping her ankles together and stared into his lustful eyes. Her chest heaved up and down with each breath. Her stomach flipped and twisted as if she were being tossed around at Mach-five.

Following him into his bedroom had been a crazy impulse.

Kissing him? Pure insanity.

But, as he pressed her back against the mattress, his hard body between her legs, she surely knew she'd lost her marbles.

His facial stubble tickled her skin as he smothered her neck in kisses, nibbling on her earlobe.

Needing to feel his skin against her fingertips, she

slid her hands under his shirt, resisting the urge to glide them into his pants so that she could cup his tight ass.

Screw it. She'd already all but attacked the poor man.

He groaned as he pressed his mouth over her breast, which was hidden behind a thin T-Shirt and bra, but he managed to find her nipple, his teeth scraping over it through the fabric.

All she wanted was her skin to be touched by his like how flames hugged a crackling log as it sizzled in a fire pit. Her lungs ached as her breath came in short pants. Her hands grappled with his clothing, trying to remove as much as she could.

He snagged both her hands, raising them over her head, pinning her down.

"What's the rush?" he asked before he bit her lower lip, not giving her a chance to respond as he kissed his way down her neck, across her chest, lifting her shirt and exposing her bra. His lips seared on the skin on the top of her breasts.

She wiggled the shirt over her head as he found the front clasp. The room blurred in the background. All she could focus on was him and how his tongue blistered her body as if she were being kissed by the sun. Fisting the comforter, she closed her eyes, letting out a moan as he rolled her pants over her hips.

The way his hands held her body reminded her of how warm water felt trickling over her aching body, only she wasn't sore but instead needed to be caressed and devoured. She might have started this tangle in the sheets, but, she gladly gave the reigns over to Ramey, who thus far, seemed to be the master at making a woman wither underneath his touch.

As they shed the rest of their clothing, Tequila let go completely, giving herself to Ramey. He played her body like the finest bow gliding across the strings of a rare violin. He was tender and kind as he gave every inch of her skin his fullest attention. He demanded nothing of her, other than with every moan or calling out of his name; she was rewarded with an encore.

Tequila didn't like to relinquish control of any situation, yet, twice today, she'd trusted Ramey, first when she got in his chopper and now in his bed. She chalked it up to being cut from the same cloth. Neither one wanted a long-term relationship. They might have different reasons, but the result was just the same.

They had an instant attraction, and when you add all the things they had in common, it was inevitable they'd end up in bed, so why fight it.

His scruffy, barely there beard, tickled the inside of her thigh. While she anticipated what came next, she wasn't prepared for the intense heat that trickled out of her body. Her insides erupted with hot pulses as she arched her back, digging her heels into the bed. She clutched his head, rolling her hips in motion with his mouth and fingers.

Her chest tightened, and she could barely breathe as she tried to control a rumble about to turn into an earthquake. She blinked, staring up at the skylight, then down at Ramey, who looked up and smiled before settling back down between her legs. His fingers and tongue massaged her in ways she'd never imagined.

And she had a good imagination.

Clutching her legs together, tugging at his hair, she groaned as her body bucked and convulsed. Her stomach tightened, quivering like a volcano as it exploded.

He reached up and twisted her nipple between his thumb and forefinger.

"Oh… my…" she said, tossing her head back and forth, raising her hips as he continued to stroke and lap at her. Her body reacted over and over again in multiple orgasms that crushed her ability to think of anything other than the sheer pleasure he brought her.

He kissed her stomach, moving his way toward her breasts, taking each nipple into his mouth, swirling his tongue over the hard nub before sucking deep. His hand still cupping her, gently stroking her as after-shocks rippled across her skin.

Nuzzling next to her, he kissed her shoulder. "Are you ready for more?"

She'd yet been able to catch her breath. "The question is: are you?" she managed to ask as she pushed him to his back, taking the length of him in her hand. His cock throbbed against her palm as she gently stroked.

"I was born ready."

She squeezed.

He let out a long, slow hiss when she brought her

tongue to the tip, her hand gliding up and down the length of him.

His hands found their way to her breasts, and he pinched and tugged at her nipples, driving her mad with desire. She found herself desperate to please him, a feeling she didn't welcome, but couldn't ignore. She'd been a selfish lover with most of the men she'd been with, taking charge, and demanding more from them. She greedily got her fill, but now she found herself in an almost panicked state, wanting to hear him groan and call out her name as she made him climax.

Only she found herself laying on her side with his fingers inside her again. Her body tightened and tingled. She tried to focus on giving him pleasure, but it proved impossible as her body betrayed her.

She tossed her head back, squeezing his shaft as she groaned.

"Jesus," she said behind gritted teeth. Her climax coming down so hard and fast she was afraid she'd spasm right off the bed. "Oh, my, God, Ramey."

She could have sworn she heard... or maybe felt him laugh.

Gripping him, she watched her hand ride up and down. There was something beautifully magnificent about his body. Besides being muscular and strong, his skin was soft, and he smelled like a late walk on the beach as the sun descended over the horizon. His fingers massaged her thigh, and his lips kissed her shuddering stomach.

"Where's the condom?" she needed to feel him inside her, but she also needed to gain some control.

"There's a box in the top drawer of my dresser." He pointed across the room.

She scooted off the bed and prowled across the room where she found a few boxes of condoms in the drawer. She pulled one out and turned.

She swallowed.

He'd propped himself up on a few pillows, one hand behind his head, the other strategically placed over himself, barely caressing.

If she had the number for People Magazine, she'd call them up and tell them she'd just met the sexiest man alive.

Ever.

Tossing the foil package toward him, she crawled onto the bed, enjoying how his eyes widened.

"Put it on."

"Yes, ma'am," he said with a deep throaty voice.

Kneeling in front of him, she watched as he masterfully covered himself. He leaned forward.

"No. Stay just like that."

He arched a brow but didn't move as she straddled him, rubbing his tip across her.

He groaned, grabbing her hips, shifting his slightly.

"I wouldn't tease me too long," he said.

She smiled, taking him in slowly, inch by glorious inch. He dug his fingers into her flesh as she rolled her hips over him, gently rocking back and forth, cupping her breasts, watching his facial expressions as she toyed with her nipples.

His hands jerked her body while his chest rose up and down, his breath raspy and short.

"You think you can do it for me one more time?" he asked.

"Do what?"

He cocked his head, taking her hand and placed her fingers where their bodies joined.

She bit down on her lower lip as he guided her motions. He propped himself up, sucking her nipple into his mouth.

"Oh, God," she whispered, riding him faster while once again she fell under the spell of his magic touch.

Before she knew what hit her, he had her on her back, legs wrapped around his waist. He fanned her cheeks with his thumbs as he stared into her eyes.

For a moment, he stopped moving.

She stopped breathing.

"You're amazing." He thrust into her with wild abandon.

She accepted his pace, grinding as hard as she could while he never glanced away. Their gaze locked with one another as she tightened her legs, feeling the ripple of pleasure tickle her toes as it moved across her body.

"Yes," she whispered, trembling in his arms as another orgasm tore through her system. One tremor after the other, vibrating and rocking her insides until she thought she might erupt.

He slammed into her and stayed deep inside for a long moment before repeating the motion.

"Just fucking incredible," he said before his mouth took hers with fury. His tongue probing deep as his entire being shuddered with release. His groan filled the room, giving her more satisfaction than she'd ever felt before with any man. She ran her hands up and down his back, massaging his shoulders gently as he slowed his motions, giving them a chance to catch their breath.

He kissed her softly, moving across her lips, cheek, and neck as he collapsed on the bed next to her, pulling her in close, spooning her.

It shocked her how neatly they fit together. Cuddling hadn't been her thing. Not that she didn't necessarily enjoy the after sex snuggle, she did, but it never felt this comfortable.

Or this good.

She let out a long sigh as Ramey pulled the sheet over their bodies.

Talk about a walking contradiction.

His fingers glided up and down her arm as he nuzzled his face in her neck. His knees tucked up against hers.

She should want to bolt from his bed, get dressed, and go about the business of…

Fuck.

"We need to check all your planes for potential tampering."

He chuckled. "I know, but let's do that after we eat those sandwiches, you started to make."

"I forgot about those," she admitted. "I am kind of hungry."

"I'm starving." He nibbled on her shoulder.

"Worked up an appetite, did ya?"

He laughed, rolling away from her and patting her ass. "I had one before, and now I'm just all that more hungry." He lifted her torso from the bed. "And after we eat and check my planes, I might want to have some dessert."

"I think you started with dessert."

He groaned, kissing her lips, darting his tongue in her mouth. "What am I going to do with you?"

"I can think of a few things."

4

*R*amey stuck his head into the engine compartment of Roxi, looking for possible tampering while doing his best to avoid the constant stare of Tequila. He'd often felt a little awkward after being with a woman if he had to spend any length of time with her after sex, but to be rendered nearly speechless?

Never.

Not Ramey.

Some would call him a womanizer, and perhaps there was a ring of truth to the statement in the sense that he had no intention of having anything other than a good time, but that was a concept he made sure was quite clear with any woman he had a short-term fling with. He never led anyone on, and he never treated a lady with anything other than respect.

And he respected Tequila, even if he wanted to

douse her body in salt, lick her, take a few shots, and then pour lemon juice all over her body.

He bent upward.

Bam!

Fuck.

He rubbed the back of his head.

"You okay?" Her sweet voice called from the other side of the room. It had this high-pitched sound that seeped into his eardrums like the hum of a perfect engine.

"I'm fine." Everything except his damn ego. Since when did he hit his head while looking at the inside of a plane?

And since when did a woman tie his stomach into tight knots? The first time that had happened was when he lost his virginity to one of the maids at his mother's place of employment. The last time had been with Denise.

He shook his head. Denise had done a number on him, and he resented that it still bothered him. Not because he wanted a woman in a forever kind of way, but because she had a tendency to creep into his subconscious, reminding him what it felt like to have his heart torn into a million pieces, and that made him crazy.

"You're not going to be fine when you see this."

He wiped his hands on a rag as he meandered across the hangar toward his Stinson 108, the very first personal plane he'd ever purchased, acting as if Tequila did not affect him whatsoever.

She had the engine cover lifted as she leaned against the nose. Her legs crossed at the ankles. God, she had sexy legs, and he could feel them wrapped around his waist as he buried himself inside her.

But the memory that took his breath away was how utterly terrified he'd been to get out of the bed and lose the feeling of her in his arms.

Not the sex part of skin pressed against hot skin.

Though mind-blowing.

But the quiet mix of their breath and beating hearts pulsating together that blanketed them with the kind of comfort and contentment that could only come from...

No. He wasn't going to go there.

"What's the problem?" he asked, focusing on the fact that someone had fucked with his planes, not the woman he wanted to fuck.

Again.

"Frayed starter wire." She tapped her knuckle against the metal. "Looks like it could be just worn."

"Only I check that kind of stuff before every flight."

"That's what I figured."

He positioned himself next to her, letting his arm touch hers like a horny adolescent. "I took her to work for about five days, two weeks ago. Haven't flown her since."

"Why not?"

"I don't want any of my planes to feel neglected, so I rotate them, giving them each my undivided attention."

Tequila shifted her weight, leaning more against

him than the airplane. A closeness he couldn't turn away but didn't necessarily welcome either. He swallowed. It was bad enough that he'd made love to her in his bed, but he either had to take her back to the base and let her go back to whatever hotel she had checked into, or let her stay the night.

"Do you have an order in which you fly them, or is it whatever your feeling that day or week?"

He ran his fingers across his chin, drawing his thumb and pointer finger together in the center. "I suppose I rotate them the same unless one needs maintenance or I'm going somewhere specific that requires a certain type of landing or takeoff."

She nodded. "Do you always fly to the base? To work?"

"No. But it's faster, so sometimes it's just about how much time I leave myself to get to work."

"Do you do any kind of check before you leave the base?"

Usually, Ramey hated answering questions in an interview. But he liked the way her voice filled his ears like the sweet sound of a perfect melody of wind and waves under the stars at the ocean.

"Standard SOP."

"Every time?"

He nodded. He'd been harassed his entire life for being a 'by the books' man when it came to following procedure for every flight, except when your job is to test the limits and help create those SOP's, better to air on the side of caution than be dead.

"Do you let anyone fly or borrow your planes?"

"I give lessons to a few people on my off time, and I've let a couple of close buddies and my little brother borrow them."

Her lips turned into a smile. "Nick said he once nearly killed both of you when you tried to teach him to fly."

He cocked his head. "The way he likes to tell the story is that *I* nearly killed us."

She laughed. "I read between the lines."

"Smart woman." He gave her a little hip check.

"Let me ask you this." She pivoted her body, leaning her side against the plane, facing him and catching his gaze. "Who do you trust the most at the base?"

"Myself."

She arched a brow.

He rolled his eyes. "Roland. He's the head of maintenance, and he works with me on a project."

"What kind of project?"

"I give kids with cancer, and other illnesses rides in my planes. I started doing it when Roland's daughter had to go through Chemo. It made her happy, and then other families asked and next thing I knew, Roland and I created a program to give sick kids rides and in some cases, flying lessons."

"That's sweet. How is Roland's daughter doing?"

Ramey sucked in his breath. "She passed six months ago."

"Jesus, I'm sorry." She reached out, curling her fingers around his biceps.

41

"Thanks."

"Is Roland back at work?" Tequila asked with a soft, tender tone.

"He never really stopped working other than the week of the funeral. Working and our project helps him with the grief." He took her hand, and held it at his side, running his thumb in circles against her palm, feeling the contrast of soft skin with that of a woman who wasn't afraid of hard work.

"I can understand that," she said softly, then cleared her throat.

He noticed tears welling in her eyes. He wanted to ask what kind of loss she'd suffered, but she spoke too quickly.

"What about the person you trust the least?"

"That's easy. Jasper, my boss."

She tilted her, narrowing her eyes. "Why? He's the one who made the initial contact with my bosses at the Aegis Network."

Ramey had met both Bain Asher and Decker Griggs, the co-founders of the Aegis Network. Stand-up men. His brothers trust them with everything they held dear.

And Ramey trusted his brothers.

"He agreed too quickly to bring you in."

"You expected him to say no?"

Ramey nodded, looking down at his hand, covering hers. The pull to be near her, and share everything with her, knocked on the back of his brain like a jackhammer. "Jasper likes to play tight to the rules, and there is no way the government is bringing in an outsider before taking it in front of an inquiry, even if a plane was destroyed or worse, I died. So, for him to say yes and make that happen makes me suspicious."

"You think he's behind this?" She put her hand on his shoulder, squeezing gently.

Ramey shook his head. "I don't believe so, but I think Jasper is hiding something."

"Like what? I can't believe, based on what I've read about your boss, that he'd want to ruin you, much less kill you."

Ramey had to agree, and he couldn't think of a single motivation Jasper could have to hurt him. "Jasper's hiding something. I don't know if it has to do with my accidents, or something else, but I've thought he'd been acting odd the last few weeks."

"Can you be more specific?" Her fingers locked behind his neck as she pressed that fantastic chest of hers against his. Her hot breath tickling his lips as she leaned in.

He reached up, prying her hands from his body and stepping back. He needed to shut this down because no way could he handle a woman spending the night in his bed.

With him.

All night.

His pulse kicked up, and his throat tightened. He never allowed himself to feel anything other than attraction and respect for a woman, and he did that by keeping them out of his personal space. His brother,

Nick, always accused him of being mean to the ladies he dated, which was only partially true and only when the lines that he'd drawn were crossed.

Only, he hadn't made any of that clear with Tequila, and he needed to right now before anything sexual could ever happen again.

And it was going to happen again.

"I'll get you the files and then why don't I drive you back to the base, or whatever hotel you're staying at and we can take this up in the morning."

Her eyes widened, then contracted to tiny slits. "I'm not leaving."

He scratched the back of his head. "Look. You pegged me as being the kind of man who doesn't do relationships, and you're right. Along with that, I don't have the woman I am sleeping with spend the night."

"Interesting choice of words. Sleeping with and spending the night," she said. "But I'm not looking for a relationship or a bed partner." She patted his chest. "When this job is over, I'm out of here and back to Florida, so you can relax."

"Good to know, but I still don't have women spend the night, so let's get you—"

"Doesn't change the fact that I'm not leaving your side. I was hired to—"

"Hired by the government and now me, so I don't need you on my six all the time."

"I work for the Aegis Network *and* your brothers said if you tried to turn me away or tried to take over, that I was hired by them to be your personal babysitter." She planted her hands on her sexy hips. "I'm not leaving your side until this is solved and if you don't want a repeat performance of earlier, fine be me. It wasn't meant to be anything other than a fling."

Ouch.

"I'm going to kill my fucking brother's when this is over."

If she wanted to stay, that was fine. She could sleep on the sofa.

He rubbed his ear, remembering the searing pain from when his mother would grab him there as a small boy.

Fuck. "You can take the bed. I'll sleep on the pull-out."

"Works for me."

5

*T*he last thing Tequila wanted to do was sleep in Ramey's bed.

Without him in it.

The entire evening, she tried to avoid the bed, by sitting at his desk, reading through all the reports he'd given her, but her eyes slowly drooped and at one in the morning, she called it a night.

She didn't sleep much, but when she did, Ramey crawled into her dreams and wouldn't go away.

She rubbed the steam off the mirror in the bathroom with the towel she'd taken off her head. Running her fingers through her damp hair, she stared at herself in the mirror. When she'd woken up, the musky smell of Ramey and their insanely, sexy afternoon, lingered in the air like a string of exotic salami in a butcher shop, strong, pungent, and wild.

After finding a shirt and a pair of sweats that fit her frame, she tip-toed into the kitchen on the hunt for coffee. However, she didn't make it past the bedroom door as she'd looked across the room and saw Ramey lounging on the sofa bare-chested with one leg peeking out of the covers as he lay sprawled out on the pull-out sofa.

She turned to make a quick escape; only she walked right into the wall. "Fuck."

"You okay?" Ramey called.

She hobbled, grabbing her toe, blood trickling out from under the nail bed. "Yeah, yeah. I'm fine."

He came up behind her, holding her at the waist. "That looks like it hurt."

"Can't say it felt good." She let him help guide her to the recliner in the family room. Putting her leg up, she glanced down at her mangled toe, with blood dripping out of the side. "I just walked into the wall. How the hell does that happen?"

"I'll get a bandage."

She glanced over at him as he walked away, wearing nothing but his boxers. His muscular legs flexed with each step.

"How about some coffee, too?" she asked.

"That can be arranged."

She turned her focus back to her throbbing toe. It didn't hurt that bad, even though deep bruises had started to form, but damn, her ego took a hit. She wasn't much of a klutz, but every once in a while, she was known for doing something stupid, like walking into a wall.

He strolled in front of her and knelt with a bottle of

peroxide in one hand and a small first aid kit in the other.

"I wanted coffee, not a dousing of pain."

He laughed as he dabbed her toe. "Your nail is loose."

"It was loose before," she said under her breath.

"So, you make it a habit of walking into things?"

She hissed as he cleaned her open wound. It wasn't big, but considering the damage she'd done a month ago, she figured the skin underneath the nail was raw.

He masterfully wrapped her toe in gauze and put medical tape around it. "I would think you can get that into a shoe."

"I'll be fine. Now, how about some coffee."

"Demanding and grumpy in the morning, aren't you?" He rested his warm hand on her ankle. His thumb rubbing circles on her sensitive skin. "Did you sleep well?"

"Well enough."

"Good, because my pull-out is the worst thing in the world to sleep on. Worse than a long trip in the back of a cargo plane."

"You were sound asleep a few moments ago, so it couldn't have been that bad."

He chuckled and leaned over her body. "I saw you tip-toe down the hallway and I saw you turn and smack your leg on the wall."

She pursed her lips. "You could have warned me."

"It happened too fast." His lips hovered over hers.

His gaze hooked on her eyes like a missile lock. "If you're going to insist on staying here with me, then we're going to have to share my bed."

"You don't sleep with women, remember?"

He growled just as his lips landed on hers. His tongue parted her mouth like a plane cutting through the clouds. The kiss was tender, controlled, sweet. He cupped her chin, angling her head back as he eased himself on top of her.

Wrapping her arms around his strong body, she drew him in deeper, her fingers digging into his back. The recliner stretched back until it lifted off its legs.

Snap!

Bang!

His teeth came down on her lips, and she felt the pinch of broken skin as his body slammed into hers, and the recliner back snapped, dropping them both to the floor.

"Shit," he muttered, pressing his hands against the hard surface, staring at her. "You broke my chair."

She raised a brow. "I'm not the one who climbed on top of me."

"No, but you didn't stop me."

She cocked her head. "Let's make one thing perfectly clear. I'm attracted to you and probably wouldn't try to fend off any advances, considering yesterday's events."

"Good to know, but it still doesn't change—"

She rolled her eyes. "How many times do I have to

tell you that once this is over, I'm out of here. Thanks for a great time. Maybe our paths will cross again, but until then, well, until then." The words flew from her mouth, but her hands gently roamed his back, caressing as only a lover would. No matter how hard she tried to deny it, she wanted more from him.

Only how much more?

And what exactly did that mean?

"Then, we understand each other."

She forced a smile when she really wanted to frown. "I'm hungry." That was a dumb thing to say.

"I think I can manage some breakfast." He rose, pulling her gently with him. "I've got frozen waffles, or I can do eggs and sausage."

"What about oatmeal? And fruit. Got any fruit?"

"Instant oatmeal and I've got some berries in the fridge. Help yourself." He stood in front of the coffee machine, pouring water into the container. It gurgled, and within minutes, the room filled with the rich smell of roasted coffee beans. Nothing better.

She went about slicing up some strawberries and cleaning off a few blueberries. He'd been kind enough to boil her water and poured it over the instant oatmeal.

"What are you going to eat?" she asked, trying to make this seem reasonable when all she wanted was to grab him and take him back to bed.

Or run.

Both sounded appealing.

Ramey had gotten under her skin in less than

twenty-four hours, and she had no idea how to handle that.

"Frozen waffles," he said as he ducked his head in the freezer before pulling out a box. "Why don't you sit?" He nodded toward the breakfast bar.

She didn't argue. And she was pleasantly surprised at how delicious his coffee had turned out.

"I've got eight interviews today, and I'd like you to be near for them," she said, holding the mug under her nose, inhaling the rich aroma.

"I'm surprised the Army hasn't pulled you off considering you agreed with their findings."

"I didn't tell them that. Besides, Bain and Griggs went above your boss, and I've been given access to the plane."

"You're fucking kidding me. When did that happen?" His eyes widened.

"I got an email about it this morning."

"Wow." He rubbed the back of his neck. "I know the Aegis Network has a lot of pull, but I'm honestly shocked."

"Last night when I was going over your notes, I found a pattern that disturbed me."

"Yeah, what's that?" He leaned over the counter, staring at her intently.

"You've got a rotator in the maintenance crew."

"Two of them, actually." He nodded

"But only one that was on during both incidents and the other two you told me about."

"That would have to Mitch Spiegel. He's a good

kid." Ramey narrowed his eyes. "I don't see the motivation."

"Well, it's something we need to pursue."

Ramey nodded. "Did you find anything else?"

"Not yet, but I will look again tonight. For now, I want to head to the base; then we can come back here around four. My equipment should be here by then."

"I don't like people here without me."

"That's what Logan said, so he's coming with them."

"I guess that's okay." He glanced at his watch. "I should probably jump in the shower so we can stop by your hotel for some clothes for you."

"My suitcase is in my car, which is at the base." She scrunched her nose. "I guess I go to work like this or wear the same clothes I did yesterday and hope no one notices."

"Or, since we're going to drive this morning, we can stop at a small boutique shop in town on the way in."

"That works," she said, raising her mug.

"Give me ten minutes, and we can be out the door."

She nodded, then eyed him as he disappeared down the short hallway to his bathroom in nothing but boxers.

Sexy.

Smart.

Seriously dangerous.

The kind of man her father always told her would come and take her away from him. She wiped her eyes and the tears threatening to break free. The only family she had left was her nephew, Grant, and now that he was off at college, she felt a pang of loneliness she hadn't experienced before.

By the time Ramey had showered and gotten dressed, she'd gathered all her belongings, along with his notes she wanted for reference. She'd also done the dishes.

Sort of a domesticated thing to do, but his house was spotless, and it was the least she could do as his guest.

The ride in his Jeep was bumpy and dusty, to say the least. She thought about asking where the top was, but when she looked around inside the Jeep, she realized he probably didn't have one, which made her wonder what the hell did he did if it rained.

It had to rain every once in a while in the desert, right?

They pulled up in front of a quaint boutique in the center of a hick town in the middle of nowhere.

"Do you need money or anything?"

She smiled. "I think I can handle buying myself an outfit."

He nodded. "I'm going to go gas up and get a soda. Want anything?"

"Water. Lots of water." She grabbed her throat. "It's so ever loving dry out here."

He laughed. "You got it."

She hopped out of the Jeep and ducked into the store, hoping she'd find something simple and she was pleasantly surprised when the first thing she saw was a pair of skinny jeans and blue short-sleeve T-Shirt, in her size. Perfect.

When she stepped from the store, Ramey had just pulled up.

"That was fast," he said.

"I'm not a shopper, so when I find what I need, I'm done."

"Looks nice."

She climbed up into the Jeep and glanced in the review mirror and noticed a white car that she'd seen on the highway a mile back.

"I noticed it, too," he said. "Whoever it is they pulled out four miles into the main road."

"Ever see that car before?"

"Nope. And I haven't been able to get a good look at the driver." Ramey reached for the gear shift.

"Wait." She jumped out of the car.

"What the fuck are you doing?"

She ignored him as she made her way down the sidewalk, glancing in a few of the shop windows. When she got five cars from the vehicle in question, whoever was driving maneuvered into the street and drove off past Ramey.

She ran down the street, jumping into the Jeep. "Let's follow them."

"Nope. I got their license plate, and we'll run it. No need to let them know we're on—"

"Like they haven't figured that out with me—"

"Maybe they have, but if we don't follow them, they might think differently."

A small SUV drove by and turned the corner tight behind the white sedan. Ramey's phone buzzed.

"You've already got someone on them, don't you?"

He looked at her and flashed a big old grin. "Let's go figure out who's fucking with my planes."

6

*T*he last thing Ramey expected when he came into work was to be shuffled off into a conference room and interrogated by his own boss.

But there he sat, at one end, while Jasper leaned over the table, knuckles digging into the wood, staring down at him as if he were a small child getting caught writing graffiti on the boy's bathroom wall.

"I agreed to the Aegis Network coming in because I knew you weren't at fault."

"So, then why are you all pissed off?" Ramey leaned back in his chair, doing his best to remain relaxed when all he wanted to do was be with Tequila and all her interviews, which was another bone of contention with his boss.

"Because you've been so goddamned paranoid lately I figured if I brought them in, they'd go over the reports and be gone because no one is messing with your flights, Ramey."

"Yes, they are, and it's not just the tests here. I had to crash land my chopper yesterday, and it looks like someone cut the rear rotor cable. Not to mention we found tampering with—"

"Your personal planes are not my concern."

"Fine. Tequila found some discrepancies and concerns here at the base."

Jasper shook his head. "You have her grasping at straws. I could have had you back up in the air next week, but now you and she are setting in motion a full inquiry, and it's not just affecting you, but the entire crew, and this new program."

"Come on, Jasper. Are you telling me you don't find any of this remotely suspicious? Faulty top-secret equipment that half the military doesn't know about, two crashes, and two near misses? Something is going on, and I think you're hiding something."

Might as well put all the cards on the table, though he left out the fact he'd been followed part of the way to work.

"Do I need to order a psych eval?"

"Did you seriously just say that?" Ramey had butted heads with his superiors before. He'd even been repri- manded a few times, especially early on in his career, but no one had ever questioned his mental stability. "I'm one of the best test pilots in the Army. I push those machines to their limit so that our pilots know what they are flying and what they can and can't do in combat. I've been in more emergency landings, take- offs, simulated crashes, than anyone on this base. What happened to me with those test runs was not your run of the mill mechanical error."

"You're on leave until this special investigation is over." Jasper stood upright, shoving the chair in front of him. "For your sake, I hope she finds something because if she doesn't, your career is toast." With that, Jasper stormed out of the conference room.

Ramey waited until his boss's footsteps faded into the background before standing. A combination of anger and confusion swirled in the pit of his gut. Jasper had always trusted what Ramey told him about his test runs, even when others questioned Ramey's reports. Jasper generally had his back.

No. Jasper always had his back.

So, what the hell changed?

"How'd it go?" Tequila's voice quieted his nerves.

That made him wonder if maybe a psych evaluation wasn't out of the question, especially considering this morning's kiss, along with the invitation to his bed.

"Not well," he admitted, turning to face her.

She leaned against the doorjamb, hands behind her back, her hazel eyes casting a warm glow across the room. Talk about inviting. The woman had a magnetic pull he couldn't resist, and hell, he tried with all his might.

"I'm on leave for the time being."

"Could be worse. They could have taken your credentials."

He cocked his head. "You're not finding much, are you?"

"What little I have found, I'm not telling anyone in this place."

"I don't know if that makes me feel better or not."

She motioned her hand toward the hallway. "Come on. Let's go to the hangar and check out what's left of the first plane and examine the one from the other day."

"I don't think anyone here is going to like me anywhere near those machines."

"They don't have a choice. As the independent investigator, I'm following their protocol, which means I'm starting from the beginning, and I get to go over every detail with the pilot."

"Now, I understand why my boss is pissed." He walked next to her down the hallway and toward the main entrance of the building, resisting the urge to touch her. "You're making them start all over."

"They hired me, and the General just happens to know Bain Asher, so I have free reign for probably a week."

"I've never understood why my brothers left the military and joined the Aegis Network... until now. Power is far and wide."

"It's not power. It's connections and communication. We work with so many different people in and out of the military that it's almost incestuous."

"That's an interesting way to put it." He pushed open the main door, and his skin was assaulted with one-hundred and ten-degree heat. He tilted his face toward the sun, taking it all in. He'd always loved hot weather, even the humid Florida heat. He had no idea how people lived in the north year round. In the infantry, he'd been stuck up in Massachusetts for six months in the dead of winter, and he hated every second of it.

"Are they going to let you bring in your own equipment, too?" he asked.

"Even if they would, I don't want to transport it back and forth. Besides, I'm not convinced that the bigger threat to your life is off this base." She glanced in his direction as she took long strides across the pavement—her blond ponytail swayed back and forth with her voluptuous hips.

"What do you mean by that?"

"The car that was following us this morning is registered to Hillary Bolton."

"Never heard of her," Ramey said.

"She's an ex-military nurse that currently works in the children's hospital." Tequila lowered her head, lifting her eyelids. "She works with terminal patients."

"There was no woman in that car." The screams of F-14's flying low, seared through the air like a knife cutting through a stick of butter.

"That doesn't mean she doesn't have something to do with this and if she's been out to your place during any of these rides—"

"I have a log of everyone who has been there during those days."

They reached the hangar where the security guard

took down their information and credentials before opening the gate.

"That's the other thing. At least five people have you pegged as being paranoid. So paranoid, they think you're borderline on losing your mind," she said after they'd walked far enough away the guard couldn't hear them.

"You've got to be fucking kidding me." He pulled open the door. "So, if they can't kill me, then they want to send me off the base in a straight jacket."

"That's a theory I can get behind."

"Wonderful," he said under his breath as he pushed back the door, letting her walk through first.

The hangar stored the remains of the sixth-generation stealth bomber he'd totaled, the one he crash landed, along with three other planes that had various problems during their test runs. Ramey's planes had been roped off, but that really wouldn't stop anyone from fucking with them, except for the security cameras.

Placing his hands on his hips, he scanned the wreckage.

"You're lucky you survived that one." Tequila pointed to the hunk of burnt metal. "According to the black box and log, you waited until the very last second to eject."

He nodded, rubbing his thigh. He remembered all too well how close he came to not seeing his next birthday.

"Why'd you wait so long?"

She'd heard the box, so he wondered why she asked, but he decided not to bust her ass and just answer.

"The initial fire was minimal. I'd shut down one engine and had disengaged the weapons system. I was five miles from the runway. I figured I could make it."

"But then you heard the whoosh of the fire intensifying. Less than thirty seconds from when you ejected, the plane exploded."

"I didn't just hear it, I could feel the plane start to break apart, and I smelled gas and oil. But honestly, I almost didn't eject."

She walked over to the plane he'd crash landed the other day and lifted the engine flap.

He folded his arms and stood there, watching her work. She was a walking contradiction between raw womanhood, feminine sensibilities, and the smartest chick he'd ever laid on eyes. He thought about asking her if she was looking for anything specific but decided to just let her do her thing.

He trusted her.

And that freaked him right the fuck out. Not because she was a woman. Far from it. Even for a short-term fling, he preferred a bright, intelligent woman who could carry her side of a conversation. He respected his brothers, and he trusted the men he worked with, so he valued and respected her talent as an ex-pilot and in her current position with the Aegis Network.

That was all fine and dandy.

Trusting she was a kind, decent, and loyal woman

that wouldn't crush his heart into a million pieces made no sense whatsoever.

He swallowed, remembering how he cried in his mother's arms after Denise had left him at the altar. His mother was one of a kind, and he had wanted to believe her when she told him that his heart would mend and he'd soon find love again. But Denise left at about the same time his brother, Nick, lost his first wife and unborn child. Seeing how it utterly crushed his brother had been, Ramey closed himself off, turning into what everyone referred to as a player. He didn't view himself so harshly. He liked, valued, and respected every woman he'd dated.

He just wasn't ever going to date them any longer than a couple of months.

Once or twice he thought about a relationship as a few women made his heart flutter, but not one of them made his palms sweat like a horny teenager at the same as he pictured long walks on the beach talking about everything and anything under the sun.

He shoved his hands into his pants pockets.

"Want to help me get this engine out of here?"

"Sure," he said. "I'll roll over the tool shed."

"Thanks." Her head was still shoved into the engine department, her ass sticking up. His fingers itched. He remembered just how good that ass felt in his hands, kneading her flesh.

She wiggled. "I can feel you staring at me."

"At least I'm not smacking you, because, you know, the thought has crossed my mind."

Glancing over her shoulder, smiling. "Let's get this engine out and then go see what we can find out about that nurse."

"I love it when you get all controlling and demanding."

"I'll remember that tonight."

He chuckled. "I'm looking forward to it."

7

*T*equila stood over the broken recliner, pressing a finger against her lips. She'd always prided herself on being a strong, independent woman that had too many things she wanted to do with her life, and a man would just get in the way.

While she put her career on hold to take care of her dying sister and her nephew, she didn't see herself settling down to be with one man. Her job with the Aegis Network certainly kept her hopping, sending her off to various parts of the world and she loved every second of it.

Even the bodyguard assignments.

It wasn't as thrilling as being a test pilot, but the reward was just as fulfilling.

"I guess I owe you a new recliner."

Ramey laughed as he tossed his keys on the table next to the door before securing it. "No worries. Besides, I bet I can fix it."

She rolled her suitcase to the side wall near the kitchen, a little unsure of how things were going to play out this evening. As much as she wanted to be in his bed, she found herself wanting to know the man. To understand what made him tick and not just the things he projected out into the world, but the things that he buried in the deep recesses of his mind.

Worse, she wanted to share hers.

"Do you want to get me the files on all the flights you and Roland took with kids from the hospital?"

"If you'll start dinner. I'm famished."

"You said you were cooking." She planted her hands on her hips and glared at him.

"I said I was grilling, which I will do, but you get the vegetables."

"The vegetables go on the grill, so you're doing those too."

"Then you get them ready." He breezed by her, stopping to kiss her cheek. "But if I'm doing all the cooking, you've got dish duty."

"I'm your guest."

He groaned. "You're going to make me be a gentleman, aren't you?"

Her cheeks warmed as he kissed her lips softly before heading toward his bedroom. She let out a long sigh and rummaged through the fridge until she found some asparagus. Always good in foil with a little oil and seasoning, and easy to grill.

"Here's everything on Project Horizon." Ramey dropped a thick accordion-style folder on the breakfast bar. "You know, we haven't talked too much about your interviews today."

"A few of your crew mentioned that over the last month, you've been paranoid and not your usual self."

Ramey tossed the steaks onto a butcher board and started pounding them. "I'll give them cautious and with good reason."

"Roland seemed to defend you the most, but even he said he was concerned for you."

"So he's told me."

"Tell me about Tim Brooks." She watched as Ramey beat the steak and then rub it with seasoning. For a player, the guy was incredibly nice, and not in the 'pick-up' kind of cute, but the genuine-I'm-a-nice-guy kind of sweet.

Ramey glanced up at her and tilted his head. "Brooks as in Captain Brooks, one of the other test pilots?"

"Is there any other man by that name on base?"

He laughed. "He's cocky, but not great under pressure. Not sure how he ever made the grade."

"He says you've got a death wish."

Ramey smiled, shaking his head before turning to rinse his hands at the sink. "I push those planes to their limits because it's my job. One I'm very good at. Brooks flies them like he's out on a Sunday morning stroll."

"So, it's safe to say, the two of you butt heads."

"No. We stay out of each other's way. He's got his test runs, I've got mine. We don't spend much time together at all."

"But there is a conflict."

Ramey shrugged. "Not on my end, but I suppose there could be since we don't like each other." He waved a beer in the air. "Brooks has never been out here."

"Doesn't mean he hasn't fucked with your planes. Not to mention, he went out of his way to answer questions I didn't ask about your mental stability."

"Now that is troublesome," Ramey said as he lifted the tray holding the steaks and veggies. "Mind getting the door? You can go over the files while I cook."

After she closed the door behind Ramey, she dove into the files. She wasn't sure what she was looking for but was careful to note days, times, people, and their connections to Ramey, the base, Brooks, Roland, Jasper, and Nurse Bolton, hoping to find some kind of pattern.

She did notice that Hillary had been to Ramey's hangar on two different occasions with a group of children as part of the medical team that supported the chronically ill. However, it seemed that Roland had made a note of her presence, not Ramey. Of the six times he'd taken kids up in his planes, the staff had been the same except for the last two times, which is when Nurse Bolton had been present.

She wondered if Ramey had any pictures from these events.

Leaping off the stool, she raced to her bag and took out her laptop. Google was her friend.

Not knowing Ramey's password to his Wi-Fi, she

took out her phone and engaged the hotspot and started image searching for various people. Got to love Facebook just for that reason.

Captain Brooks didn't have much of a Facebook page, thankfully. His image banner was a beautiful sunset taken from a plane. His profile image was a picture of him, his wife and two kids. The rest of his page was kept private, so unless they were 'friends' Tequila wouldn't be able to see anything else. She started down the list, entering names into the Google search, but didn't find much of anything until she entered Hillary Bolton's name.

The woman didn't have a significant social media presence, but she did have a few pictures and one stuck out like a sore thumb.

The door to Ramey's house creaked open, and the smell of perfectly cooked beef filled her nose and sent her stomach growling, reminding her of how little she'd had to eat that day.

"Come look at this," she said, tilting her computer.

Ramey set the food down on the counter and leaned over her shoulder, his hand resting on the back of her neck.

"That's Brooks, and the girl he's with looks vaguely familiar, but not exactly sure who she is."

"That's our Nurse Bolton."

"Really? That's odd, don't you think?"

"Not to mention, Brooks is married," Tequila said.

"He's in the middle of a divorce, but I don't know the details." Ramey moved into the kitchen, pulling out a couple of plates, utensils, and a bottle of red wine. "Shall we switch?"

"Works for me." She polished off her beer, pushed her computer aside, and opened the veggie foil. "I think we need to make a trip to the hospital in the morning and have a little chat with Nurse Bolton."

"I need to go there anyway." Ramey pulled out the stool next to her, poured two glasses of wine, then dug into his steak. "One of the little boys I took up last time has had a relapse, and I promised his dad I'd come to visit this week."

"Perfect." She raised her knife and sliced into her piece of meat. The smell of garlic and pepper tickled her nose, threatening to make her sneeze. "But before we go, I want to run a few tests. Hopefully, your bother will be here soon."

"He texted me and said he'd be here by eight. He had to take a side trip to help with an assignment. And before I forget, he's crashing here tonight on the sofa before he takes off in the morning."

She swallowed, trying not to choke on her food. "And the pilot that's bringing him? Where is he staying?"

"I have a room in the hangar with a full bath." He tilted his head, catching her gaze with his soft blue eyes that twinkled with a mix of mischief and something akin to concern. "How well do you know my brother, Logan? Or Nick, for that matter?"

"I've met them both in the Aegis Network office.

I've been in briefs with them but never worked with either of them. Yet."

"Logan is going to harass the shit out of me, and you, when he finds out, you're sleeping in my bed."

She coughed. "I don't think it's such a good idea with my co-worker in the next room. It was unprofessional of me to hop in the sack with you, to begin with."

A slow smile spread across his face as he leaned closer. His fingers tugged at her hair, lifting her chin. "First, he's not your boss; he's my brother." Ramey pressed his lips against hers in a quick kiss. "Second. What's done is done."

"True. But we don't have to flaunt it in anyone's face."

He licked her lips, sucking on the bottom one for a second. "It's not flaunting, and I don't give a shit what my brother thinks, I'm just warning you that he will harass us."

"Wonderful," she whispered, leaning into his muscular frame. "I should push you away and go to a hotel."

"But you're not going to." He cupped the back of her neck. "You're making me break all my rules."

"Some rules are meant to be broken." She circled her arms around his body, slipping her hands under his shirt, running her fingernails across his lower back, enjoying the deep groan that escaped his lips.

"My rules are to protect myself from women like you." His hot breath tickled her ear.

She cocked her head back and stared into his lusty eyes with a thick layer of vulnerability that made her gasp. "Women like me? What does that mean?"

He took her hand, kissing her palm before placing it on the center of his chest. "Women who might actually be worthy of my love."

8

The second the word love accidentally tumbled out his mouth, Ramey felt his heart squeeze and his stomach rumble like a roller derby on crack. He stared into her wide-eyes, wishing he could come up with some sarcastic remark that would not only negate what he'd just said but make them both laugh.

Ding! Ding!

They both jumped as the intercom system rang out.

He released her and walked across the room. His hand trembled as he raised it to the panel next to the door.

"Ramey here."

"Logan here. Open the damn door."

"Say, please."

"Screw you," Logan said.

Ramey laughed. Bantering with his brother would be just what he needed.

He frowned.

That banter would include talking about the woman he'd not only expected to share his bed tonight but the women he'd used the lo—nope. He wouldn't go there. He hit the code to open the outer door. Before turning to face Tequila, he took in a deep calming breath.

Her back was to him as she picked at the food on her plate and sipped her wine.

Could he be a bigger moron?

He maneuvered to the other side of the counter, bringing his plate with him so he could finish the last few bites before starting on the dishes. If he let her near the sink, his mother would not only yank at his ear; she'd probably smack him upside the head.

"Do you know the guy who flew your equipment out here?" Ramey asked, trying to dial things back a bit.

"Yeah. Kyle Ludwig. Ex-Air Force Pilot."

"Did you know him in the military?"

She glanced up from her plate. No smile. Just that wide-eyed confused look he'd put there with his stupid confession that couldn't possibly be true.

"I'm just asking."

"Yeah. I knew him." She nodded.

"What's he like?"

"Kyle doesn't talk much. He more like grunts. He's new to the Aegis Network, as in the last month. I helped recruit him. He's a good man." Her tone had changed from playful, to a monotone rendition of a professor giving a lecture on organic chemistry as he read from his own index cards.

"Logan said he'd be fine sleeping in my spare quarters."

"Why do you have a room out there anyway?"

Ramey shrugged. "It was there when I bought the place."

The front door flew open, crashing against the stopper on the wall. "The least you could have done was meet us inside the hangar and help with our luggage." Logan stepped into the family room, tossing a duffle bag on the sofa before taking another bag from a man whose shoulder girth had to be the size of the state of Texas. His thick neck sported a black tattoo of a crow.

Ramey set his plate next to the sink and pointed to Tequila. "Don't even think about doing the dishes."

She tossed her hands up as she swiveled on the stool, rotating to in the other direction. "Hey, Logan. Hey, Kyle. How was the flight?"

"Safe and uneventful, unlike flying with my little brother."

She laughed. "I'm not sure I want to get in an aircraft with him ever again."

He poked her shoulder as he walked by. "And to think I might have let you fly one."

"Promises, promises," she said.

Ramey took his brother's hand, noting the arched brow and the curve of a slight smile before yanking him in for a brotherly hug. "It's good to see you."

"Mia sends her best. I've got pictures of Abigail in my bag for you." Logan stepped back, resting both hands on Ramey's shoulders.

Logan wasn't the tallest of the Sarich brothers, but he did have a good three and a half inches on Ramey, making him, the runt of the litter.

"You're looking old there, little brother," Logan said.

"You wish, old man."

"The insults could go on forever." Logan slapped Ramey's back. "Kyle, this is Ramey and blah blah blah."

Ramey shook Kyle's hand and tried not to wince as he squeezed so hard Ramey thought a bone might crack. Usually, Ramey would take this as an alpha male squaring off against another alpha, marking their territory.

But the slight shift in Kyle's body and a twitch of his mouth, let Ramey know something else.

Tequila had moved and now stood next to him. He watched…no he gawked as Kyle took her hand with delicate care as if he were picking up a precious piece of art and leaned in, kissing her cheek.

He flexed his fingers, trying to rid himself of the painful shake Kyle had given him, but more importantly, he bit back a smile. Straight men could learn a lot about how to treat a lady from their gay counterpart.

"We brought your equipment inside. Shall we go set it up?" Kyle asked.

"That would be great. I'd like to run some non-flight tests tonight." She turned to Ramey, placing her hand on his biceps, making his head spin. "If that's okay?"

"Go right ahead. I'll be out in a minute." He locked gazes with her for a long moment. He felt his brother's stare.

God, Ramey wanted to take her in his arms, kiss her hard, claiming her as his, but he didn't think that would go over too well. Besides, she wasn't his, and he shouldn't even be thinking like that. He raked a hand through his hair and watched as she and Kyle left his home, shutting the door behind them.

About five seconds later, Logan burst out in laughter.

"I don't see what the hell is so funny."

Logan slapped Ramey's back. "I knew the two of you would have the hots for one another. But I never expected to see you fall for her so hard and fast."

"I haven't fallen for her," Ramey muttered as he shuffled off into the kitchen, hearing his mother's voice screaming at him to pick up his feet. "I just didn't expect to have you and that goon as house guests, along with her."

"She's sleeping here?" Logan helped himself to a glass of wine as he leaned against the counter.

Ramey took his glass and raised it. The brothers clinked and then Ramey chugged half of it. "She's been instructed by someone…" Ramey pointed a finger at his brother. "…to be on me, twenty-four-seven."

"With you. Not on you." Logan smiled wide. "We all

thought you'd make her sleep at that dive hotel at the edge of town."

"Now that would be silly, considering she needs to look at the planes and I have a perfectly good spare room in the hangar." Ramey set his glass down, turning his back. He focused on the dishes, not the amused stare his brother gave him. He and his brothers shared a bond that went far beyond having the same parents.

Beyond being brothers in arms.

They shared almost everything.

Right now, he'd wished he'd told Logan about Denise years ago.

"You seriously didn't make her sleep out there, did you?"

Ramey laughed. "She's ex-military. I'm sure it wouldn't have creeped her out too badly."

"Operative words there are *wouldn't have.* So, where is she sleeping?"

Ramey wiped his hands on the dishtowel before topping off his glass. He swirled the red liquid, raising it to his nose, inhaling the full-bodied scent. "Last night, she slept in my room, I slept on the sofa."

Logan lowered his chin. "Mom would be proud?"

"Not really," Ramey admitted. "What do you know about Tequila?"

"Jesus, you have fallen." Logan set his wine on the counter. "I was just busting on you since I knew you'd like her, but you more than like her."

"Shut up and tell me what you know. Like why'd she leave the military? Any recent breakups? Family?"

"I need to sit down for this."

Ramey followed his brother into the family room.

Logan paused in front of the broken chair. "Do I want to know how that happened?" He pointed to the recliner sprawled out in three different pieces. He shook his head. "Never mind. I don't want to know." He sat on the sofa, pushing the bags to the floor. "I don't know much other than she's one hell of a pilot with a huge personality. I've been told by others, not her, that she left the military because of a death in her family and she's got a nephew at the Air Force Academy."

Ramey positioned himself in the wingback chair kitty-corner from his brother, looking out the window into the hangar. An odd thing to have, but currently it gave him comfort to see Tequila hooking up instruments to his planes and examining them more closely than they had yesterday.

"She says she's like me. Restless. Not wanting to settle down. But I don't see a reason behind it."

Logan let out a long breath. "Not everyone needs to have some traumatic event in their life to bring them to that conclusion. I mean, before Mia came back into my life, I had no reason for not wanting a serious relationship."

Through the window, Tequila caught Ramey's gaze. She smiled, then ducked her head back into Roxi. Typically, anyone touching his Roxi without him present would make his skin crawl.

But all she did was warm his body like a mug of hot buttered rum.

"Your reason was you had always been in love with Mia, but after dad died, and what that did to mom, and then you hurt your shoulder, you just got scared and ran. And fast. You just didn't know what you were running from. Neither does Dylan. But Nick? He knew the pain of love and loss better than anyone."

"Yes, he did. But he's so happy with Leandra and excited, though nervous as all shit. That said, he goes gaga over Abigail so much he makes me look like a bad father."

Ramey stared at his brother. "You're a great father, and you know it."

Logan nodded, but his expression turned serious, like when their father would sit them to talk to them about how to treat a lady. "I know you got hurt badly at West Point. But hearts, they do heal, if you let them."

Ramey sucked in a deep breath. "Excuse me?"

"I don't know her name, or anything about her, or what she did to you. We all respected your wish for privacy, but come on, man. Do you think we didn't know?"

"Did mom tell you?" Ramey pushed the air out of his lungs and sucked in as much fresh oxygen as he could. His heart hammered against his chest so hard it rattled his teeth.

"Mom knows?" Logan tilted his head, arching a brow. "Wow. I had no idea. And she still never eased up on trying to marry you off? Wow. That's something."

"That's because she was always at her happiest with dad." Ramey scratched the stubble on his cheek.

"And with raising us," Logan said.

"We were a handful, weren't we?"

Both men rubbed their ears and laughed.

Logan leaned forward, resting his forearms on his thighs. "Whatever you're feeling right now for Tequila and all the fear that goes with it, don't push it away. Give yourself a chance to fall in love again. Trust me when I say, it's a life changer."

Ramey dropped his head back and closed his eyes. He'd loved once. And he'd lost. The old cliché hounded him like a swarm of bees after a pre-pubescent little shit kicked their nest. Ever since his two older brothers had gotten married, he had to admit he'd thought about what it would be like to share his life with someone.

Someone who understood his restlessness and his career.

Mostly someone who was like him.

It begged the question: could two people who didn't think they wanted to be in a committed relationship be in one with each other? Would that work?

"*D*o you want to talk about it?"

Tequila cringed at Kyle's question. She'd first met him during a training exercise her second week in flight school. He reminded her of a cross between the grim reaper and a lost puppy. Rough around the edges, but sweet as pie.

And so gay.

"Not sure what you are referring to?"

He wiped his greasy hands on a bright orange towel before snapping it at her pant leg. "If he weren't as straight as straight could be, I'd be hitting on him."

"You really do like coming off as a psychopathic murderer to straight men, don't you?"

"It's even more fun when they find out I bat for the other team, only that one in there picked up on it right away. He's not just hot, he's smart, and I give him a 'thumbs up' because he's not homophobic. But you're changing the subject, sweetheart."

Flipping over a large, sturdy bucket, she sat down and let out a long sigh. "I hate to admit it, but I like him. I mean the kind of like that makes someone think about those forever kind of things."

"That's not so bad."

"I just got Grant into college, and while he's doing well, I still need to focus on him."

"Grant is a grown man."

"He's barely eighteen and lost both his parents in a two-year span. I can't go off and—"

Kyle put his steady hand on her shoulder. "Grant is in Colorado. In school. You can date if you want."

"I know that. But hello. Ramey lives in the middle of the desert, isolated from the world, and you know I'm never leaving Orlando. So, what the fuck am I doing letting myself have feelings for a man who is a bit of recluse with a wild streak in the air that could get him killed?"

"Wow." Kyle pulled up a bucket. "You've already slept with him."

She blinked a few times. Kyle was the closest thing she had to a best girlfriend. Hell, he even took her shopping. A necessary evil she hated.

"I even initiated it, though he would have eventually." She looked up at the ceiling. She couldn't ask for anyone more perfect than Ramey. It wasn't about his looks, though they did help. But she could see into his soul, something she suspected no one had ever cared to do before. He had a bravado stance and acted as if nothing got to him, but in the short time she'd known him, she saw what made him tick. "A long-distance romance would be disastrous."

"It wouldn't be easy, that's for sure. But there's more. Spill it, girl."

She locked gazes with Kyle. His eyes conveyed genuine kindness and unconditional friendship.

"He mentioned something about how I was the kind of woman he could fall in love with."

"Before or after you jumped his bones."

She cocked her head. "After. Like fully clothed, day after, at the dinner table, conversation with eyes locked. Then you assholes showed up."

"Oh my. That is something to ponder now, isn't it?"

She didn't get to respond that statement because Ramey and Logan strolled into the hangar.

"Find anything?" Ramey asked.

"We did," Kyle said as he stood. "And you're not going to like it."

"Lay it on me," Ramey said, offering his hand to Tequila.

When her skin touched his, a warmth glided across her body. It felt like he'd wrapped her in a fuzzy blanket where she could curl up in his arms and be protected from all that was bad in the world. His fingers curled around hers as they followed Kyle.

"We found metal shavings in the oil system of the helicopter, and you've got a slow leak in the plane you named Roxi," Kyle said as he stopped in front of the aircraft she and Ramey had crash landed yesterday.

"I'm meticulous about maintenance," Ramey said.

"More like anal retentive." Logan climbed inside the bird.

"You're one to talk. You probably have an SOP for changing your daughter's diaper."

"You would not believe what comes out of a baby," Logan said as he tapped one of the controls. "Was this glass cracked before the accident?"

With her hand still entwined with Ramey's, Tequila peeked her head in. "I remember it being cracked when I got in."

"Seriously?" Ramey leaned over her shoulder. "I thought that happened when we landed."

She looked at him, shaking her head.

"Fuck," he muttered.

"I'll spend tomorrow doing a full service run on all the planes," Kyle said.

"Aren't you and Logan going back to Orlando?" Ramey asked.

"Nope. We're here for as long as we're useful." Logan smacked his brother on the back. "And before you say anything, Mia would make me sleep on the sofa if I didn't stay and help your sorry ass out. Which reminds me." He pointed to Kyle. "You've got the room at the top of the stairs over there. I'm still stuck on the sofa. And these two love birds get a nice big, comfy king size bed."

"At least I won't be able to hear them," Kyle said with a hearty laugh. "But I feel sorry for you in the room right next to them. I mean my girl here, when she gets excited in a plane she—"

"Shut up, Kyle." Tequila took her free hand and punched his arm.

"Ramey howls when he's—"

"Screw you both," Ramey said under his breath.

"I think fuck you both is more like it," Tequila said, squeezing his hand with all her might. She didn't want to hurt him but instead sought his comfort, and he seemed to understand as his thumb ran a soft circle on her skin.

"Oh, God. You two are perfect for each other. I can't wait to tell mom." Logan waltzed in front of them, looping his arm around Kyle's shoulder, both of them glancing back with stupid ass smiles on their face.

Tequila swallowed. The last thing she needed was to be the topic of conversation with anyone and Ramey's mother.

9

*R*amey stood at the end of his bed in his boxers, contemplating on if he should follow his routine and drop his shorts before climbing into bed. Or leave them on.

He glanced toward the door, Tequila still in the bathroom. Talk about bizarre situations. Not only was he going to sleep in his own bed with a woman for the first time, but he had his brother and a stranger as houseguests to boot.

He blinked as she padded into his bedroom wearing his shorts and T-shirt. Her hair damp from a shower. He took in a deep breath, inhaling the scent of peach mixed with the fresh smell of spring. Her nipples puckered under the fabric of his shirt.

"Do you have a side preference?" he asked, still gawking at her.

"I don't know. I generally sleep alone and in the middle." She stood next to him. The heat from her body filtered through the air, landing on his skin with a splash.

"Well, we both can't sleep in the middle."

"I'll take the side closest to the bathroom." She stepped around the mattress and pulled back the comforter. "This has to go down as one of the weirdest things in my life."

"I've been called a lot of things, but no woman has ever described sleeping with me as weird."

"That you know of." She fluffed the pillows and leaned against them, smiling like a princess with devil horns that you couldn't see.

God, he loved that look.

"Point taken." He practically flung himself on the bed like a toddler, crawling up to the headboard and kicking back the sheets. "Sorry about my asshole brother."

"Sorry about my dipshit friend."

Ramey slid his leg over, catching her foot with his. This was uncharted territory, and the hardest part was that it didn't bother him.

Scared him? Well, hell, yes.

"So, do you want to know about the woman who made me never want to have a long-term relationship?"

"If you want to tell me, I'll listen."

He rolled to his side, kissing her shoulder, letting his fingers dance up and down her soft arm. "Denise, a classmate at West Point, and my girlfriend during my senior year, left me standing at the courthouse with a marriage license in my hand."

"As in she just didn't show up?"

He dropped his head to the pillow, gazing into Tequila's sea-like eyes. "Denise showed up. She said she wanted to tell me in person why she couldn't marry me."

"At the courthouse?" Tequila lowered her chin as her eyes widened. "She couldn't have called and asked to meet you before?"

"I never asked that question, because she showed up, told me she was going to marry her ex-boyfriend from home in a couple of months. She told me she confused the excitement of our relationship for love and that while she'd always think fondly of me, she needed to walk away."

"Holy fuck. What did you do?"

"Nothing. I just stood there like an idiot and watched her walk away. I sat on a bench in the hallway for hours, dumbfounded. Eventually, I went back to my dorm. Graduation was a week away, and my family was coming, so I sucked it up and acted as if nothing happened until that August when a classmate showed me Denise's wedding picture in the newspaper. It turns out the ex from home happened to be some hot shot, wealthy socialite. That was it. I was done with women in a long-term kind of way."

"I would be too after that. Where is this Denise now, because I kind of hope she's miserable?"

He smiled. "I have no idea, and I honestly don't care anymore."

"Good on you." She cupped his face. "But she still controls your love life like a puppet master."

He chuckled. "I think someone is changing that and I have no idea how to cope because you honestly scare the crap out of me."

Her wide smile squeezed his heart and covered his skin in goosebumps.

"The feeling is mutual. As in the scary part."

"You turn," he said. "Why don't you want a partner in life?"

"It's not that I don't want one. But I've never been in love. I've tried, but every man I've ever been with only made me feel lukewarm."

"I think I do more than that."

"You do, but other than loving my family, I'm not sure I even know what real love looks like. I think I'm incapable of falling in love."

Ramey brushed his lips against hers in a swift, passionate gesture. "I doubt that." One of the reasons he'd developed so many rules had been because he knew he could fall in love again if he wasn't careful. "Something has you spooked, and whatever that is, it's keeping your heart under lock and key."

"I suppose it has to do with how heartbroken my dad was over my mom."

"What happened?" Ramey asked, drawing her into his arms, sprawling his hands against her back, feeling her arch into him. He wanted to know everything about her, right down to who her first-grade teacher was and what kind of ice cream she loved.

"She died a few hours after I was born."

Ramey jerked his head back. "I'm so sorry."

She let out a long sigh. "I wish I could have had at least one memory of her."

"I can understand that. May I ask what happened?"

"She started hemorrhaging shortly after I was born and the doctors couldn't stop it."

Ramey knew what it felt like to lose a parent at a young age. His father had been what Ramey aspired to be like. He always tried to emulate him when he'd been alive. But to have never known him, that he couldn't imagine. Nor could he comprehend what it must have been like for her father.

"Did your father blame you?"

"Never. Not once. He was a great father, but he never got over her. Sometimes I'd see him in his office, looking at her picture, crying like a baby. He always tried to hide that from me, but I saw it. I tried fixing him up with my teachers, but he never dated."

"My mom hasn't dated, and my dad has been dead for thirteen years. She's spent all that time trying to marry us off so she can have grandbabies."

Tequila shivered in his arms.

He held her tighter, kissing her temple, understanding how that statement could bother her.

Only the shiver bothered him more.

"Where is your dad now?" he asked.

"He passed away. I was still in high school. My sister and her husband moved home to take care of me."

"I'm sorry." Ramey left out a long sigh. So much death for one person to deal with.

She tilted her head toward him with water in her eyes. "My mother died, breaking my father's heart. I watched it. Lived it. My sister's husband died, leaving behind her and their son, Grant. Then two years ago, my sister lost her battle with cancer. Grant wasn't even sixteen yet."

He fanned his thumb across her cheek, wiping away the tear. His heart beat so fast it hurt. The mere thought of losing his brothers crippled his ability to think straight. They might not see each other every day or even talk every day, but they were his world. What mattered.

"I don't want to die and leave someone heartbroken to live out their days in some empty shell, simply going through the motions. I don't want to cause anyone that kind of grief," she said.

Cradling her head on his shoulder, he rolled to his back, holding her as tenderly as he could. He'd never thought of it that way. He didn't want to love because he didn't want to get hurt again. Tequila didn't want to hurt anyone. She'd rather live her days alone than be the cause of anyone's pain.

At that moment, Ramey knew that he didn't want to go a day without her in his life.

Yet, he was going to have to let her go.

His mother's voiced pecked at his mind; *it's better to have loved and lost, then to never know what it feels like to have the world, even if for only a short moment.*

This was his moment. In a day or two, it would be over.

He held her, caressing her arms and back, pressing his lips against her forehead with sweet tender kisses. Her body relaxed into his, and he figured she'd fall asleep there, and that was okay. He could give her whatever she needed right now.

"I didn't know that's how I felt," she whispered.

"Now you know, and that's a good thing."

"I'm not so sure about that." She lifted her head. "This is a really bad idea for both of us."

"Probably," he said, staring into her gaze that sucked him right in.

"We should stop before either one of is in too deep."

Too late for that, but he'd never let her know. "We've only known each other for a couple of days. We both understand each other, more than anyone else we've been with, which is what is scary. Makes us vulnerable, but when your job here is done, and you go back to Orlando, we won't be but a nice memory to draw on in a sea of shit."

She smiled, letting out a short laugh.

And his heart rejoiced.

And he was so fucked.

"Nice way with the words," she said.

"Someone had to lighten the mood." Revert back to sarcasm and diversion. Good plan, only he knew it wouldn't work on his insides that had turned into a puddle of mush.

She got on her knees. "I don't think this lightens it,

but it should have a positive reaction." She ripped her shirt over her head, tossing it to the side. Her blonde hair bounced over her shoulders and her nipples puckered.

He wanted to kiss them. Caress them.

Love them.

Fuck. He was toast.

He swallowed the lump in his throat as he leaned in, cupping the soft mounds and bringing them to his lips. He knew her leaving was going to hurt and that was something he'd have to deal with.

Alone.

He'd never let her see him hurt.

But tonight was going to be different.

He knelt next to her, kissing his way up her long, soft neck and nibbling on her chin until he landed on her plump lips. Gently, he glided his tongue between them. His fingers fanned over her hard nipples, barely grazing them.

She tried to reach inside his shorts, but he batted her hand away. There would be no power struggle. This wasn't going to be a romp in bed designed solely for primal release. If he was going to have to let her go, he wanted one night that could be something close to perfect as one could get.

He pushed her onto her back, kissing her mouth. She tasted like chocolate mint and felt like warm honey drizzled over his skin.

Her hands sprawled out over his back, fingers digging in. Her legs spread open as he settled himself on top of her. Visions of what a life could be like with her tortured his mind. He could see them sitting at the beach. Taking long airplane rides up and down the coast. Laughing.

Loving.

Making love to her was such a bad idea.

He shoved his tongue deeper in her mouth, swirling every inch. He pushed himself hard against her and was rewarded with a loud moan.

As he removed her shorts and rid himself of his own, he took a moment to admire her body. The way it glistened under the moon and the stars peaking in from the skylights humbled him. But it wasn't just her body that was perfection.

It was the woman inside. As he looked into her eyes, he could see the real Tequila. The woman who cared for everyone in her family, putting herself last.

Tonight, she'd come first.

He lifted her foot, kissing her ankle, gliding his tongue up the sweet curve of her calf, looking into her heavy eyes, filled with desire.

For him.

It took his breath away. Made him dizzy. The room spun as if he'd had too much to drink.

Of her.

All he wanted right now was to satisfy her every desire.

He buried his face between her legs, kissing and lapping as her hips rolled and her hands dug into his scalp. His name floating from her lips to his ears. He was lost in her. This was like nothing he'd ever experienced.

And he'd experienced some pretty amazing sexual encounters.

But Tequila made him drunk.

He smiled against her, enjoying her sweet, succulent juices. He could tell she was close, and that made him even more intoxicated.

All of a sudden, she pushed him away.

He blinked, looking up at her, worried he did something wrong, but then she tossed him on his back, straddled him, reaching over him toward the nightstand. Before he could truly comprehend what was happening, she'd covered him in the condom.

He groaned as she lowered herself on top of him. It felt like he'd stepped onto the beach on the most gorgeous of sunny, warm days. He sucked in a breath and could have sworn he tasted the salty ocean air.

Holding onto her round hips, he kept her movements slow and controlled, though it wasn't easy. She tossed her head back, moaning, cupping her breasts as she rode over him.

His chest heaved up and down with his labored breath. He squeezed her hips tighter, rocking her a little faster, feeling her tighten around him. She looked down at him. Her gaze filled with passion. Her body withering with desire. Rocking back and forth and up and down, she cried out as she bent over, her hands on his chest, nails digging into his skin.

He grabbed her face, holding her gaze as he thrust

himself into her. He searched her eyes as her climax spilled out, jerking her body. He swelled inside her and burst seconds later, still staring into her captivating gaze, groaning out her name.

He had no idea how long they explored each other's intense stare, other than it lasted for as long as they needed to catch their breath. He pulled her chest down to his, rolling her body to his side. Her arms and legs draped over him like a soft and cozy snuggle.

He was turning into a sap.

Soon to be a slightly heartbroken sap, because people didn't fall in love in a couple of days. That took weeks or months of getting to know one another.

He kissed her forehead and closed his eyes, ignoring the voice in the back of his head telling him he'd fallen so far deep in love he'd never be able to see past it.

10

Tequila climbed out of the Jeep in the parking lot of the Horizon Hospital parking garage, her cheeks still warm with embarrassment.

Not only had her revelation about why she couldn't, or didn't, allow herself to love anyone, shocked her.

But she'd said it out loud.

To Ramey.

Then she made love to him.

She needed this case to be done, and then she needed a good shot of whiskey. Better yet, make it a bottle.

Her and Ramey might be cut from the same cloth, but no one, including her, should be trying to sew it together, especially considering how distant Ramey had been all morning.

Distant and cold.

"We probably shouldn't be seen going in together,"

Ramey said. His hands firmly planted on his hips as he looked toward the tall building.

"Why don't you and Logan go in first? Check-in and visit with the little boy you promised to see, and Kyle and I will go up in about ten minutes, asking for the nurse." Tequila tried to ignore the pang of hurt she felt when Ramey barely even looked at her.

"I'm a tough sell on being a reporter," Kyle said, looping his arm over Tequila as if he knew she needed a friendly embrace.

"I think the question will be more of why are there, two reporters," Logan said, stepping up next to his brother. "But we use the buddy system. We have no idea what we're dealing with."

"Agreed." Ramey turned his head and pointed at Kyle. "You watch her back, got it."

"Got it," Kyle said.

Great. He goes from being an asshole to a stupid Neanderthal in two seconds flat. Not that his comment meant he cared. No, it was probably just him showing his true colors.

Ramey glanced over his shoulder and gave her a slight smile. She nodded, but it didn't make her feel any better.

"What crawled up his ass?" Kyle asked as he nudged her across the parking garage and away from Ramey's Jeep. Just in case.

"Me."

Kyle opened his mouth, then, like the smart man he was, quickly snapped it shut.

"I got too close too quick and spooked us both, but it's for the best."

"You haven't even given him a chance."

She stopped to let a car drive past before making her way to the skywalk. "We live like two thousand miles from each other, and that isn't the biggest issue. Now let's drop it and focus on the plan."

"I'm still not convinced that Brooks and this Nurse Bolton are trying to discredit or kill Ramey."

"Right now, it's the only lead we have and after interviewing Brooks, and his team, well let's just say that Brooks has it in for Ramey on many levels."

"What's Nurse Bolton's motivation?"

"Don't know yet, but maybe we can get some insight—"

Click!

Click!

Cold metal pressed against the back of her head.

Out of the corner of her eye, she saw Kyle's eyes roll to the back of his head as he collapsed to the ground, Nurse Bolton standing over him.

Before she could calculate the risks of going for her weapon, Captain Brooks had taken it from her.

"What did you give him?" Tequila asked.

"Nothing that will kill him, yet," the nurse said.

"Move." Brooks pressed the gun into her back, pushing her back across the pavement.

She watched as the nurse, with one other people she couldn't see, load Kyle's body onto a gurney and into an ambulance parked near the elevator.

"Where are you taking him?" she asked, assessing the area for people. Hopefully, someone saw what happened, which might help Logan and Ramey in finding her and Kyle.

She swallowed. Her experiences in combat had been in the air, not on the ground.

"Don't you worry about him. Now get in." He shoved her into a dark sedan with tinted windows. She hoped it was a government vehicle, which would be stupid on his part.

She suspected that he wasn't that stupid.

Slipping into the back seat, she saw Jasper Marlin. Her heartbeat kicked up.

"Don't look so surprised."

"Shocked is more like it."

The engine of the sedan kicked over and Brooks pulled out of the parking space nice and slow. She noted the ambulance wasn't too far behind them as they eased out into traffic.

"You've been a pain in my ass the second you stepped into my office."

"Why'd you invite me then?" She folded her arms, glaring at the Lieutenant Colonel.

"When Ramey asked for a special investigation, I fought it. Hard. But I had to bring it to the review board. I practically begged them not to, that Ramey was just stressed and maybe needed a vacation. But no. They think, like everyone else in this God forsaken place, that Ramey is fucking Superman."

"You want to kill him because you're jealous of him?

That's kind of lame, don't ya think?" She mentally slapped herself. Baiting the man wasn't going to make the situation any better, but she couldn't help herself.

"Tsk. Tsk." He shook his head. "I'm not jealous at all. I respect Ramey. He's the best test pilot we have, and the problem is everyone knows it. You see. I need him out of the way; whether that be because he's dead, or deemed crazy, I could care less. I just need Brooks to be testing the sixth-generation planes so I can sell one."

Her eyebrows shot up. "You're going to do what?"

"You heard me." He tapped her knee. "Now pull out your cell phone and tell him to meet you back at his place."

"He won't believe I left without him."

Jasper drew his lips in a tight line. "Tell him if he's not there in an hour, with his brother, you're a dead woman."

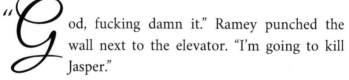

"**G**od, fucking damn it." Ramey punched the wall next to the elevator. "I'm going to kill Jasper."

"No, you're not," Logan said, squeezing his shoulder, but it didn't calm Ramey one bit. If anything, it made him see red.

He should have never left Tequila alone.

Hell, he should have known it was Jasper.

"Watch me," Ramey muttered.

"We're not going there half-cocked. We need a plan and—"

Ramey's phone buzzed. He glanced at the number. "It's Dylan." He tapped his phone. "Where you at?" he asked his little brother.

"I'm forty-five minutes away," Dylan said. "Lucky for you, I was at Area 51."

"Can you get here?"

"I can, and I've got a couple of buddies coming with me. Tell me where to meet you."

"At the edge of town where the dirt road to my place starts. There's a country store—"

"I remember. I'll be there."

Ramey ended the call feeling a little more confident about the situation now that he'd have two of his brothers at his side, but that didn't help the fear that crept into his mind and body, taking over his ability to compartmentalize. He'd been on many ops where his job was to rescue people his family loved and cared for.

Mother fucker had Tequila.

And threatened to kill her.

No one threatened to kill someone he loved and got away with it.

His heart squeezed as he stepped into the elevator. His chest tightened, and it became difficult to breathe. He swallowed, but it didn't help.

How could anyone fall in love with someone in a couple of days?

Okay, his brother, Nick, could. But not Ramey.

Nope.

Yep.

Fuck.

"We're not going to let anything happen to her," Logan said.

He tried to hold on to that concept as they made their way through the hospital and back out to the garage. For the next twenty minutes, as he sped through town, he did his best to focus on the sound of Logan's voice and the plan that began to form, but every time there was a lull, his mind shot back to Tequila.

And Kyle.

He had to protect them both.

The Jeep skidded to a stop in front of the small store. The owner waltzed out, opening the side door, nodding to Ramey.

"A private room in a convenient store?" Logan asked, arching a brow.

Ramey shrugged. "I like to play cards sometimes."

"Mom would kill you if she knew you gambled."

"Oh, please. It's a pick-up game of Texas hold 'em, and the stakes aren't very high. Not like you've never played the game."

Logan laughed. "Mia would wring my neck. She hates gambling."

Ramey shook his head. "Now that is weird coming from a hacker."

"Ethical Hacker. There is a difference."

The sound of sand and dirt being kicked up by large tires caught Ramey's attention. A dark suburban parked next to his Jeep. Checking the area, he made sure no one else was in sight. He'd picked this spot, in part because they could go over the plan in the privacy of the poker room as well as he could see for miles around making sure no one was watching.

He looked to the sky.

Well, no one except those who had access to the... "Can you call Mia or her brother and have them hack the satellite—"

"On it," Logan said.

Dylan stepped from the vehicle, all six-foot-four of him.

"He looks taller to me every time I see him."

"Maybe you've started shrinking," Logan said.

"That's funny, old man," Ramey said as he met his little brother half way and gave him a brotherly slap on the back. "What brings you to the desert that you didn't call me ahead of time?"

"I just got here an hour ago, and I can't tell you."

"Of course you can't, Mr. Highest-Security-Clearance," Ramey said. "How does the youngest one climb up the ranks faster than anyone else?"

"Because I'm smarter than all of you put together." Of all the Sarich boys, Dylan had been the most reserved in his demeanor. The quiet, gentle giant.

"Hey, baby Dyl," Logan said, giving him a brotherly punch on the shoulder.

"Jesus, will you ever stop with that shit." Dylan punched Logan back. "You know I can take you, right?"

"That will be the day." Logan laughed.

"Enough of that. Let's go devise a plan that will save my woman." Ramey winced the second he heard what came out of his mouth.

"What the fuck did you just say?" Dylan paused dead in his tracks. "Your woman?"

"Yeah, don't let Tequila hear you call her that," Logan said. "I suspect she doesn't like being considered anyone's property."

"She's not my property," Ramey muttered, wishing he could take the words back. Not because of how she might respond, but he didn't feel like taking the razzing from his brothers.

"Please don't tell me you went and fell in love." Dylan visibly shook like a dog ridding itself of water.

"Heavy like," Ramey said.

"It's love," Logan teased. "And it's contagious."

"God, I fucking hope not," Dylan said.

11

*T*equila sat in the ambulance next to Kyle, her finger pressed against his wrist. His heartbeat slower than it should be, but it was steady. His breath was shallow, the low rumble of a snore made her think they'd given him either an intravenous anesthesia drug or a heavy dose of pain killers.

Nurse Bolton leaned against the ambulance doors, gun in hand. Tequila knew she could easily overpower the woman, but her real concern then was the firepower that Jasper, Brooks, and the man dressed in a black overhaul suit who'd been hiding his face, held, and whether or not they valued the nurse's life. Considering how high the stakes were, and the chain of command, leaving the nurse as low man on the totem pole, Tequila figured Jasper would put a bullet in the nurse's head and not bat an eyelash.

Jasper and Brooks stood in front of Ramey's chopper, whispering while the unknown man tinkered with the engine.

That couldn't be good.

She tilted her head to the left, then the right, trying to get the right angle so she could see the man's face, but no luck. She couldn't even assess his size since he'd been hidden behind the helicopter the entire time.

"You do realize you're either going to end up dead, or rotting in prison for the rest of your life." Tequila continued to contemplate a potential escape, but with Kyle unconscious, that would be difficult.

"You're the only bitch that is going to die." Nurse Bolton didn't even glance over her shoulder.

"We're all going to die someday; only I think I'm going be around to see the sun rise again."

This time the nurse turned her head and let out a short laugh that sounded more like a pig squealing. "I'm going to enjoy watching you crash and burn."

"So, that's the plan? Make me fly away in a doomed aircraft?"

"You, Ramey, his stupid brother, your unconscious friend. It's a pretty perfect plan."

"Not even close," Tequila said, trying not to laugh. "Ramey and I are about the best damn pilots known to the military. We'll survive."

"No, you won't, and it will be a tragic accident due to mechanical failure and human error."

"We don't make mistakes."

Nurse Bolton shook her head. "Stupid girl. Don't

you see? Ramey has been unstable for a while. It's just too bad he has to take all of you with him."

In the distance, the humming of Ramey's Jeep caught Tequila's attention. She squeezed Kyle's hand and climbed from the ambulance.

Nurse Bolton raised her weapon, pointing it at the side of her head. "I won't hesitate to shoot you."

Tequila ignored the statement, focusing on the Jeep racing across the desert. She glanced at her watch. Precisely one hour from the time she called and barely meeting the deadline Jasper had set for her untimely demise. She forced her lips into a tight line, keeping them from curling upward. Ramey and Logan wouldn't wait that long to show up unless they had a plan.

Nurse Bolton's cold and clammy fingers curled around Tequila's biceps.

Tequila squelched the urge to bat the gun pointed at her face away but figured that might end badly. It annoyed her that she was being watched over by the likes of Nurse Bolton.

The Jeep came to a stop about fifteen feet from where she stood. Ramey stepped from the driver's seat, his face hard. "You okay?" he asked.

"I'm not dead, yet." Tequila gave a quick nod, eyeing Logan as he moved around to the front of the Jeep, leaning against the hood, hands folded across his chest. Behind her, the sound of boots crunching in the hard desert ground sent a shiver up her spine.

"Glad you could join the party," Jasper said,

standing on the other side of her. "Now step away from the Jeep, walk slowly toward me, hands in the air."

Ramey and Logan raised their arms, palms facing Jasper and took a few steps when suddenly both men paused. Logan went rigid.

Ramey's eyes widened. "What the fuck? Roland?"

he desert sun had to be playing tricks on Ramey's eyes because no way could Roland have anything to do with a plan to steal a sixth-generation aircraft and sell it to their countries enemies.

"Sorry, brother." Roland continued to close the gap, carrying an assault weapon in his hands.

"Don't call me, brother." Bile crawled up his throat.

"It's nothing personal."

"You've got to be fucking kidding me," Ramey said under his breath. "You've been fucking with my planes? Trying to kill me?"

"Not all the planes. Brooks fucked with a lot of them."

Ramey made his way over to Tequila. "Where's Kyle?" he asked. He needed to rid his mind of the betrayal standing behind him, with a gun to his back, and focus on how to make sure they made it out alive.

"They gave him something to knock him out, and he's been out cold in the back of the ambulance for the last hour."

He glanced in his brother's direction, making eye-contact for a brief moment, before they both scanned the area searching for any sign of Dylan or his team. Being in the middle of nowhere made it difficult to make a surprise entrance, which was the entire reason Ramey liked living there.

Currently, he was re-thinking that philosophy.

He was rethinking a lot of things, but that would all have to wait.

"Why, Roland?" Ramey asked.

"Does it matter?"

"It does to me." As they walked past the ambulance, Ramey glanced inside the bay doors. Pretty stupid on their part to leave Kyle unattended, unless what they gave him was slowly killing him, a thought that made the hair on the back of Ramey's neck stand at attention.

No sooner did he have that thought, did the nurse walk toward the ambulance and climbed inside.

"Money. Lots of money," Roland said.

That made no sense to Ramey at all. Roland's family was wealthy, a fact most people knew. It's how he could get the best doctors and treatment for his little girl, even though it hadn't saved her life. It's also how they funded their project. Ramey glanced over his shoulder. "You'd betray your country, me, for more money?"

"I've got nothing else to live for," Roland said.

That, Ramey could understand to a point.

"You should be asking why Brooks and Jasper are doing it, though."

"Does it matter?" Ramey tossed Roland's words back at him as he stopped in front of his helicopter. He turned around, facing his captors. Tequila on his right. Logan on his left. Dylan, hopefully somewhere close.

Roland stood like an Airman would who was on high alert, guarding something. Brooks and Jasper, on the other hand, were in a relaxed position, which Ramey could exploit.

"It might matter to you," Roland said. "Go ahead Brooks, tell Ramey why you're betraying your country."

"This is stupid," Jasper said, shifting his weight. "Get in the helicopter."

"Hey," Logan said, raising his hands to the side. "I've got nothing to do with this, so if I'm going to die today, I'd sure as shit like to know why."

"Me too," Tequila said. "I know that Jasper wants to sell the plane and the weapons system to the Koreans and needed his guy on the test runs to do it, but I have no idea why."

Jasper took a few steps forward, getting in Tequila's face.

Ramey tried to come between them, but Roland stopped him with his weapon. Ramey glanced between the metal object stabbing him in the gut and Roland's face.

He still struggled with believing Roland could turn on him. He understood grief and watched what losing an unborn child had done to Nick. He knew people snapped all the time. But the man, staring him down with a stone-cold face of a killer, hadn't snapped.

"I was well on my way to becoming a General, but

because of politics and one mistake, I was passed over and ended up here, in this God-forsaken land to oversee idiots like Ramey. It's a bullshit job and a demotion with no chance of moving up. When a Korean operative approached me with this opportunity, I jumped on it."

"You know, the Koreans will torture and then kill you after you deliver the plane," Logan said.

Jasper laughed. "They need me. Unlike my own damned country."

Ramey's fingers twitched. He wanted nothing more than to be able to land a quick jab on Jasper's nose, breaking it. "Killing us isn't going to make the problem of my tests flights go away."

"Oh yes it will," Brooks said, with a stupid smile on his face, one that Ramey would like to remove.

"Not all the paperwork has been filed, so making a few adjustments, so it appears poor Ramey was unstable, burned out, and incompetent, won't be so hard.

"That is the funniest thing I've ever heard." Ramey's laugh was cut short when Roland raised his weapon.

"This is about the time we should be telling you to climb into your chopper, but I'm not going to do that." Roland whistled, then turned his rifle on Jasper.

"What the fuck? Get that thing out of my face."

"Nope," Roland said.

Brooks raised his weapon, pressing it to the back of Roland's head. "You're a stupid man."

"I'm the smartest one here," Roland said with a smile.

"You can put a bullet in my head. I don't care. But if you do that, Jasper here takes a good fifteen rounds before I drop, and if you think Ramey is going to kill you, you've got another coming. He'll make sure you get court-marshaled and spend your final days in prison as a traitor."

"That's an excellent point," Ramey said. "I'd put the gun down, Brooks."

In a flash, Brooks aimed at Logan.

Ramey sucked in a breath as Brooks pressed the weapon at the center of Logan's forehead.

"Oh fuck," Tequila said.

Ramey turned his head to see Kyle step from the ambulance with Nurse Bolton following behind. Too many weapons pointed at his people. Where the fuck was Dylan?

"I'm getting tired of this," Jasper said. "Put down the fucking gun, Roland. You're not going to kill me."

"You're right, I'm not," Roland said, nodding. "But they might."

One hundred paces due east of the hangar, toward the main road, the desert sand flew through the air as three armored military vehicles approached.

The hum of helicopters in the distance echoed off the tin hangar.

The second Brooks shifted his stare; Logan disarmed him.

Out of the corner of Ramey's eye, he watched Kyle disarm the nurse. Roland held the rifle against Jasper's chest, whose face had grown pale.

"Interesting turn of events," Tequila said, her voice rolling over his ears. Sweetest thing he'd ever heard.

"Do you feel like you were left out of the action because I do," Ramey said.

She nodded.

"I can't be left out." Ramey cocked his fist and swung at Brooks. The crackle of his knuckles hitting Brooks square on the cheek never sounded so good.

"No one threatens my brother."

Logan laughed. "I'm not Baby, and I'm not in a corner."

"What?" Ramey shook out his hand, feeling the warmth of Tequila's fingers around his arm, immediately calming his pulse.

"It's a line from the movie Dirty Dancing," Tequila said.

"Dirty what?" Ramey asked.

"A chick flick from the eighties. Something Mia makes me watch every once in a while. Not that bad, actually," Logan said as he took Brooks by the arm.

"Don't get any ideas about chick flicks. I don't do cheesy romance anything." Ramey waggled his finger at Tequila.

"Hey, there's Dylan." Logan pointed toward the lead armor vehicle that stopped near the ambulance.

"I thought he only had the couple of guys we met at the convenience store, not half of Delta Force, or whatever organization our little brother is working for these days," Ramey said.

"Those are my people." Roland held out his rifle. "Hold this for a second."

Ramey took the weapon, still not sure what to think of Roland or his role in this insane conspiracy.

Roland unzipped his overalls, then ripped open his shirt, uncovering a wire.

"You mother fucker," Jasper said in a low growl. "You…You…set me up?"

Roland laughed. "You think I'd turn on my country and my brothers? I might have lost the one thing that meant the most to me, but that doesn't mean I don't have anything or anyone left to love."

"How long have you known about their plan?" Ramey handed the weapon to Tequila, staring at his friend.

"I knew something wasn't right a few months ago. Once I figured it out, I didn't know who I could turn to, so I went off base. I kept rechecking your test runs, and I kept finding things that had been tampered with. I fixed what I found and documented everything. We didn't have enough, so when I got the call today, they put a wire on me and here we are."

"Sorry, I doubted you."

"Did you think I'd not only commit treason but betray you?"

"You were holding an assault rifle on me."

"I wouldn't have shot you," Roland said. "And by the way, while they thought I was making sure your helicopter would go up in flames, I fixed the leak, but you need to replace a couple of parts."

"Thanks for the heads up." Ramey watched Roland walk away, with Brooks and Jasper, handing them over to the military police. Ramey looped his arm over Tequila.

"Is that your other brother?"

"That's baby Dyl."

"He's tall, handsome, and dreamy."

"He's an asshole. I'm the better catch."

Logan laughed. "I can't wait to call mom."

Ramey growled. "I don't know that there is anything to tell mom yet."

"Better figure that out right quick." Logan slapped Ramey on the back before jogging off to meet Dylan.

Ramey let out a long breath as he set his hands on her soft hips. "I guess your job is over now."

She nodded.

His thoughts wondered to things like family and love. He'd be lost without his brothers, their wives…his mother. God, his mother, was their rock. The strongest woman he'd ever met.

Tequila, in a weird way, reminded him of his mother.

"Do you have to head back to Orlando right away?" he asked.

"Probably pretty quickly."

"Do you want to head back quickly?"

She smiled. "Not particularly."

"Why is that?" The idea that a woman could reduce him to a pile of nerves like a little school-boy with his first crush bothered him.

But having her walk out of his life scared him more.

"I don't understand why or how I ended up caring for you so much, but you've changed the way I view everything in my life."

Her hands glided across his shoulders, fingers massaging gently as she leaned into him. Her heart beat against his in a perfect pattern.

"I don't understand it either, but I want to test you out."

He laughed. "So, we're taking each other out for a test run."

"Something like that."

"What if I told you I've got six months before I re-enlist and I might not?"

Her smiled widened. "I know a great organization that would love to have you."

"We're doing this relationship thing, aren't we?" He didn't need to wait for an answer because it wasn't a question.

She fit in his arms.

And in his life.

His last flight.

EPILOGUE

SIX MONTHS LATER...

*R*amey rolled his Jeep to a stop in front of his brother, Nick's house, who lived a few doors down from his brother Logan, in a quaint little suburb of Orlando. He shut the engine down and turned off the lights. "Let's do this."

"You make it sound like we're facing the firing squad," Tequila said, her hand resting on his thigh. She'd been more than he'd ever bargained for and in a good way. The love they had for each other gave him the same feeling as when he'd been a test pilot. She filled more than a void.

She made his life perfect.

Ramey laughed. "We sort of are, considering what we have to tell them." The front door swung open, and his mother waved. "And there's my mom."

"Your mom scares me a little."

"She scares me a lot." Ramey stepped from his car, jogging around the hood, and opening the passenger side door, helping his bride from the vehicle. "She's not going to be happy we eloped."

"That's what scares me, but no way could I have done a big wedding."

"Me neither." Ramey placed his hand on the center of her back as they headed up the walkway.

"All my boys in one place," his mother said with her arms stretched wide. "I hope you can stay longer than Dylan."

"When does he have to leave?" Ramey wrapped his arms around his mother, holding her tight. Growing up, she'd always been there for him, even when she should have tossed his sorry ass to the wolves.

"Tomorrow afternoon." His mother stepped back, cupping his cheeks.

God, he hated that almost as much as when she tugged at his ear.

"You should see Dylan with Tyler. Quite comical."

"I can imagine," Tequila said as she hugged Ramey's mother.

"Then hurry before Nick takes his son back. He's terrified Dylan is going to drop him."

Ramey laughed. "That's funny coming from Nick considering he dropped Dylan twice when he was a baby."

"I know," his mother said. "I thought Logan would be the overprotective father, not Nick."

Ramey stepped into the family room where Logan sat on the floor, Abigail climbing all over him, while Mia sat behind him on the sofa. Across the room,

Dylan awkwardly held Tyler, bouncing him on his legs as the boy giggled and Nick hovered.

Leandra, Nick's wife, leaned against the wall near the opening to the dining room. "Just in time," Leandra said. "Dinner will be ready in fifteen minutes."

"Sorry we're late. We had some paperwork to take care of at the bank." Ramey stood behind Tequila, circling his arms around her middle, resting his chin on her shoulder. She pressed her hand against his, and he wondered who would be the first to notice the matching rings, or if he'd actually have to come out and announce it.

"What kind of business would you have at an Orlando bank?" his mother asked as she settled on the sofa next to Mia.

"Tequila lives here, ma, remember?" Ramey knew he should just come out and tell everyone their news, but part of him was scared to death, and the other part was going to enjoy their shocked faces.

"Of course, I remember." His mother tilted her head. "And you live in New Mexico."

He could tell she tried not to scowl and forced a slight smile, though the sarcasm wasn't lost on anyone.

"I can't imagine doing a long-distance relationship," Logan said.

"I can't imagine doing a relationship period." Dylan lifted the baby. "Please, I love your boy, but will you take him now?"

Nick quickly bent over and scooped his son into his

arms. "The right woman is going to come along and sucker-punch you right between the eyes."

"I don't have the time or the inclination," Dylan said, leaning back, clasping his hands behind his head. "I'm deployed more for more than two-hundred days in a year, and when I'm not deployed, I'm in undisclosed areas doing stuff I can't talk about. So, even if there was a perfect woman for me, she'd be miserable."

Ramey took a deep calming breath. "Being married tends to change your perspective on your career."

"Right," Dylan said with a sarcastic tone. "That coming from the man who isn't married and is about to re-enlist."

"Wrong on both accounts, little brother." Ramey held up his hand, showing off his silver wedding band. "And, we bought the house over on Ellington, which was the banking we needed to deal with."

"And Ramey took a job with the Aegis Network," Tequila added.

His mother flew off the sofa like a lion on the attack.

"Ramey Jordan Sarich," she said, pulling both him and Tequila into her arms. "If I cared about weddings, I'd be so angry right now."

"Well I'll be damned," Logan said. "When did you tie the knot?"

"A couple of weeks ago." Ramey gave his mother a kiss on the cheek, grateful his ear was left unharmed. Nothing worse than having it tugged on in front of your wife.

Wife. As in he was married.

He still wasn't used to it, but he loved the way it made him feel like he was going Mach five over the mountains.

"Now all I need is for Dylan to see the light," Ramey's mother said.

"Ma, stop, okay? Besides, shouldn't you be pressuring them to have more grandbabies now that they've gotten… excuse me while I gag a little…married?"

Ramey's mother marched across the room and tugged at Dylan's ear.

"Ma. Seriously?" Dylan winced.

"Marriage isn't so bad, baby Dyl. But let's hold off on the discussion about babies. Not ready for that." He took Tequila's hand and was about to kiss her when he noticed she was chewing on her fingernail.

"We don't have to discuss it, but it's happening," Tequila said.

"I know. Someday in the future, like we talked about," Ramey said, tugging at her hand. "I told you my family got all weird about babies."

"You've got to be the dumbest man on the planet," Nick said, laughing. "Back that conversation up and listen to what your wife just said."

Ramey cocked his head, staring into Tequila's warm, caramel eyes, her finger still in her mouth. "What am I missing?"

"The baby thing. It's happening now. As in, I'm pregnant. Now."

"I think I need to sit down," Ramey whispered.

Thank you for taking the time to read *The Last Flight.* Next up in the series is *The Return Home,* which is Dylan Sarich's story! You can download it today! *Sign up for Jen's Newsletter* (https://dl.bookfunnel.com/ rg8mx9lchy) *where she often gives away free books before publication.*

Join Jen's private Facebook group (https://www.facebook. com/groups/191706547909047/) where she posts exclusive excerpts and discuss all things murder and love!

ABOUT THE AUTHOR

Welcome to my World! I'm a USA Today Bestseller of Romantic Suspense, Contemporary Romance, and Paranormal Romance.

I first started writing while carting my kids to one hockey rink after the other, averaging 170 games per year between 3 kids in 2 countries and 5 states. My first book, IN TWO WEEKS was originally published in 2007. In 2010 I helped form a publishing company (Cool Gus Publishing) with NY Times Bestselling Author Bob Mayer where I ran the technical side of the business through 2016.

I'm currently enjoying the next phase of my life...the empty NESTER! My husband and I spend our winters in Jupiter, Florida and our summers in Rochester, NY. We have three amazing children who have all gone off to carve out their places in the world, while I continue to craft stories that I hope will make you readers feel good and put a smile on your face.

Sign up for my Newsletter (https://dl.bookfunnel.com/ 6atcf7g1be) where I often give away free books before publication.

Join my private Facebook group (https://www.facebook.com/

groups/191706547909047/) where I post exclusive excerpts and discuss all things murder and love!

Never miss a new release. Follow me on Amazon:amazon.com/author/jentalty

And on Bookbub: bookbub.com/authors/jen-talty

NEON SASS

PAINTING SASS

Boxsets

LOVE CHRISTMAS, MOVIES

UNFORGETABLE PASSION

UNFORGETABLE CHARMERS

A NIGHT SHE'LL REMEMBER

SWEET AND SASSY IN THE SNOW

SWEET AND SASSY PRINCE CHARMING

PROTECT AND DESIRE

SWEET AND SASSY BABY LOVE

CHRISTMAS AT MISTLETOE LODGE

THE PLAYERS: OVERCOMING THE ODDS

CHRISTMAS SHORTS

CHRISTMAS DREAMS

Novellas

NIGHTSHADE

A CHRISTMAS GETAWAY

TAKING A RISK

WHISPERS

Made in the USA
Columbia, SC
16 February 2020